Turtle Mountain Mystery

Miss Lillian

Order this book online at www.trafford.com
or email orders@trafford.com

Most Trafford titles are also available at major online book retailers.

Printed in the United States of America.

ISBN: 978-1-4669-3033-9 (sc)
ISBN: 978-1-4669-3032-2 (e)

Trafford rev. 04/19/2012

 www.trafford.com

North America & international
toll-free: 1 888 232 4444 (USA & Canada)
phone: 250 383 6864 ♦ fax: 812 355 4082

PROLOGUE

JOEL GOT OFF THE bus in the little town of Willis, near the Wyoming and South Dakota border. His mother, Marge Moss, rushed up crying and hugged him. He was out on parole. She was still shocked at his six month prison term for selling meth at the college where he had been awarded a scholarship.

After arriving home, Joel walked the floor while telling his mother everything. After being home only one hour, he said, "Ma, I have to go." She reluctantly agreed, and as he started his car, she thought, "He keeps insisting that he was set up, but there is little I can do to help." Marge, as a single mother, worked in a local cafe for many years. Everyone in the little town was so shocked to learn of Joel's behavior.

Joel drove east looking for the meth lab where he had worked for one week. He remembered sneaking a peek through a small opening around a pipe. He could see a hill shaped like a turtle with trees forming the turtle's head. As a teenager he had seen this same turtle while hunting antelope with his father, who had since passed away. He drove for three hours straight stopping only for gas, candy bars, and pop.

As a chemistry student Joel had been approached to work during spring break for a sum of $8,000; he needed the money badly. His mistake was partying too much one night and telling a friend his wild story. He was sure that's why he was arrested. When he told the officers who approached him and who was working there, everyone laughed. He said he had been in a van with covered windows and at night was driven there where they slept in an underground lab, like a dormitory with eight other students for a week. All the others denied it and had their own alibis for the week. The judge sentenced Joel to six months in the state penitentiary in Sioux Falls, South Dakota. Joel was just barely 21 years old, but that was old enough to be incarcerated in the state pen.

For the past six months now he had studied maps trying to remember exactly where the meth lab was located.

Joel had driven many miles from home on a dusty gravel road. He knew the land well, but found it to be deceiving—like a desert. He drove on and on and finally he saw the turtle off in the distance. It was now nearly dark as he came to the end of the gravel road. Ahead a dirt path led in the direction of the turtle. He drove to the edge of a cliff, got out and looked up trying to determine where the lab was located. After resting for a while in his car he got out again, carefully looking at the ground, remembering rattlesnakes were thick in this area.

The sound of an approaching pickup caught his attention. Two people got out; he recognized their voices. They asked if he was lost. Joel said "Yes, and asked for directions to the nearest town." One of the two approached Joel and asked if they should know him. Joel replied "No, I don't think so. I came here hunting with my dad once years ago." One of them casually came toward him with a shotgun pointed downward, "Looking for a den of rattlers," they both said. Joel never knew what hit him as the shotgun nearly blew him in half. One said, "Is this the one out on parole?" "Yep" was the only answer. They threw Joel in the car, one following while the other drove Joel's car a mile away to a private dump ground. They pushed the car over the hill into the dump site by hand. The two then came back in the dark with cans of lye and a tractor. They threw lye inside and outside of the car. The tractor scooped dirt over the car and it soon looked like all the other junk cars piled there.

2 WEEKS LATER

CHAPTER 1

LORINDA HUNG UP THE phone and thought "Oh God, I don't have time for this now, what made me say "Yes?" Her mother had started out with "Lorinda you have not been home longer than three days-Christmas or Thanksgiving—for three years; "How come?" Lorinda sheepish answered "I guess I'm so caught up in my own life, ah, There just does not seem to be enough hours in a day for me, I want to do so much and just making a living any more takes up most of my time."

"Do you need a vacation? Good food, good company, and lots of time to paint."

It ended up with "Sure Mom." Lorinda thought I'm 47 and still a country girl at heart. Oh, yes, she had a nice split level home, fixed up like a doll house, flowers everywhere, carefully picked rummage sale finds. Everyone who visited said she should have been an interior decorator. A beautiful yard, a retail sales job plus she liked to write, things. Sometimes she actually sold them and then there were her paintings—not spectacular, but she had actually sold a few. And then there's Ed, the man in her life right now. She must have gone through 25 men in the last 15 years after her divorce. Why doesn't Sears have a catalog of men-tall, dark, handsome, kind, trustworthy, will take care of you? HA! Ed came and went; she thought he missed her after a week or two, so he would show up, usually after he has had a few drinks. Ed had lots of money, but he wouldn't let her touch a thing in his messy house. "Eccentric" would be good word to describe Ed.

Her name is Lorinda Kemp— too much trouble to change back to her maiden name after her divorce—and she has a wonderful son and daughter-in-law living close by. Having the same name as her son seemed important at the time.

Mom O'Malley wanted her to come home to the western South Dakota, barren prairie ranch she called home all her and Lorinda's lives, to do chores while her dad went pheasant hunting for a week with her, brother Tom.

Molly O'Malley was born on this ranch, After she married Frank they bought the ranch from her folks some 50 years ago-3,000 acres of never, never, land with cows, rattlesnakes, horses, cactus, and very little water.

Actually, Lorinda looked forward to this visit; she lived 400 miles away in Sioux Falls, eastern South Dakota, where trees grow abundantly and grass stays green until winter, not burned by the hot August weather out west. She loved the ranch and secretly liked doing chores. Lorinda called her boss and asked to take a week off from her job selling clothing. He reluctantly gave permission, if she had the fall line of clothing lined up. She laughed "I've had it planned out since August, my girls know what goes on sale from the summer line, but I already called them about waiting until this unseasonable warm fall weather changes. I will be back before it turns cold." Lorinda started packing, long hair in a pony tail—shorts and a tank top and she was still sweating like a pig, as she loaded her car with paints, typewriter—casual clothes and two dressy outfits. Of course, Ed drove up, "I thought we could go out to eat. Where are you going?" She had not seen him for two weeks, no calls, no explanation. Standing in her driveway, sweaty clothes, tendrils of hair sticking out, she lost it. "Ed, do you know the song, Hit the Road Jack, come back no more, no more? Well, let's just change the Jack to "ED". I'm so over you!" Ed drove off laughing "You will be sorry, and you will miss me." Lorinda thought, What's the matter with me? I suddenly don't care about anything or anybody—boy I do need a week of peace and quiet, no stress. Little did she know that the coming week would be a test of every emotion including her devout belief in a loving God. Lorinda felt as if she was flying down the highway, her new car was great, big payments and all, but what the hell, she liked that phone number on the window that said "Call—your warranty covers everything!"

She made the trip in one day, stopping only to eat. As soon as she got west of the Missouri River she felt at home. The ranch house was on a hill and no matter what direction you looked you would see her parents' land. The only tree in the yard was the one Lorinda planted as a

4-H project when she was 12 years old. The tree strip behind the house consisted of Russian Olive trees and a few brave Elms.

Lorinda's parents were not rich by far, but they were comfortable. Her job here would be to start the tractor and take a big round bale of hay out to the cows every day and to milk the one cow for household milk and cream. The baby calves her dad bought at the sale barn thrived on the old cow's milk.

Mom O'Malley had a bad knee, but still took care of her chickens. At 69 years old, she still had little grey in her hair and her perfect skin was still regal looking. Tall, thin, she loved to cook and still baked homemade bread every week.

Frank O'Malley was a lively 71, tall grey-haired. They both hugged Lorinda as she got out of her new car. Frank was loading his own shells for hunting and Molly was making supper fit for a queen, just as she always did when her daughter came for a visit.

It was time for Lorinda to do the evening chores. Old "Katie Cow" stood still while she was milked milk to feed the various Holstein pail calves. She started the old tractor with a tine on the back and she was off to provide hay for the 150 stock cows and four horses.

Frank left just as it was getting dark to travel to her brother's place 50 miles away. He planned to stay overnight playing with his grandchildren, then off to eastern South Dakota to hunt pheasants.

Molly and Lorinda settled down with coffee after supper and started to catch up on each other's lives. Lorinda chattered away about how excited she was about her son, Seth, and his new wife, Amanda, who is expecting their baby in the Spring. She described Ed's dumb-and-dumber—ways and added, "I guess I've had enough of Ed to last me forever. Molly caught her up on the gossip about the neighbors, most who live between 5 to 10 miles away in this "big country". A new man, from Texas, bought the Olson Ranch to the west. He didn't know a damn thing about ranching but was trying to learn. Frank helped him with many ideas on what works here and what don't work. Frank and Molly had invited him for home cooked meals. She said slyly, "He's about 50, no wife, and I think he's divorced and, get, this, he has lots of money.

She said that Vanna and Dale Schultz are still rolling in money, working night and day on their huge registered Angus ranch. They had no children of their own, but treated and thought of us neighbor kids as their own.

Mary and Lester Pringle still lived here; their boys are in their forties and still lived at home. They raised rodeo stock and traveled all over the country selling saddles as well as furnishing stock, bucking horses, brahmas, and bull dogging steers. Mike and Don Pringle enjoyed the freedom of traveling, spending their winters making all kinds of leather bridles, halters, and saddles. Actually their quite famous, and supposedly very rich men, but liked to stay home for Mary's cooking and no responsibilities for keeping up a home or cleaning. Molly went on to say in a flat voice "They ask about you often, Lorinda, I guess there all right, on Saturday they go out drinking and dancing, on Sunday they're always in church.

She went on "The Drakes, like dad and I are still struggling to make a living off this unforgiving land. Their girls are scattered all-over the country. Ted and Betty were in education and it paid off as both of the girls have wonderful jobs." Molly said that she and Frank should have put more effort into Lorinda and Tom getting an education, although you both seem to be doing all right. Lorinda shook her head "Mom, Tom and I both hated school, Yeah, I know we were both "A" students, but all either of us could think about was getting on a horse and chasing cows." "This ranch was our life."

CHAPTER 2

MARGE MOSS WAITED FIVE days before giving up and finally went to the sheriffs' office. She told him about Joel being home only one day and taking off. She said "I believe something has happened to him, he would have called me by now. Trying very hard not to cry, could you help me?" He simply shook his head, "Dear God, I wish I could help, but technically he has jumped parole. Even though I hate doing this, I have to turn this in. I will put in my report that Joel is a good kid. Also, I will put out a missing person report." He said kindly "Ah, is it possible Joel just couldn't face this town or you and well ah your "Dad". Marge said "I know what my Dad is saying, that I have to face it Joel is good boy, gone bad, and that he took off to hide somewhere." Marge hurried from the office while the sheriff was still trying to reason with her.

At home she sat down to think "Surely, something has happened to Joel; I can feel it in my heart." Joel had told his mother so many things, including the name of his prison counselor, Blake Denton, Joel told Blake everything, that he knew he did wrong, but others had been there too. Marge took a chance and called the prison counselor. Blake listened to Marge's concerned story and agreed to visit her the following weekend. Joel had been a model prisoner and Blake felt as if something had gone very wrong. Even though it would be a long drive, across the entire state, Blake said, "I will see you Saturday afternoon about 2:00 or 3:00, if nothing comes of this at least I can say I have seen Mount Rushmore, something I have always wanted to do and I want to follow up on some things Joel told me. Please don't get your hopes up. I just feel I don't know that something seems fishy about Joel's sentence."

CHAPTER 3

FRIDAY MORNING

Morning arrived pretty early for Lorinda; time to milk, feed calves, and lots of other chores. She looked at the beautiful sunrise and realized that she loved this place, so isolated and peaceful. Molly had a huge breakfast ready-bacon and eggs, the works. It was wonderful to be home and not have to cook her own food or actually worry about anything. It was like reading a storybook—not real, but relaxing.

Molly said, "After dinner, let's drive over to Vanna's; I know how much she misses you." Lorinda thought to herself how, when she was a little girl, Vanna would have her come over for a tea party and they would talk like two adults, Lorinda cherished those memories. Mostly she looked around at Vanna's beautifully decorated house, imagining her own future home. Vanna had unique ideas and was so much more modern than Lorinda's mother—she actually wore slacks. Molly wouldn't be caught dead in slacks, and she had the same curtains up for 30 years.

Vanna changed things around every year. Lorinda knew Vanna; had more money but Mom could have done some of those things like wallpaper or at least adding some knick knacks. Molly's couch used to be an old army cot with a blanket thrown over, thank God, she had at least bought a nice living room set a few years ago. Lorinda had not a doubt that set would be there forever just like the curtains. At 47 Lorinda still was like a little girl playing house, she loved to redo her house and yard. She spent hours planning new paint, wallpaper, and how to use the things she got at rummage sales and flea markets. She even designed a manmade stream through the back yard with little tables and chairs scattered around. Years ago she started with a small water garden leading up to a bubbling stream complete with goldfish swimming under a bridge. Doing everything herself was the most satisfying work she had ever done and, yes, she built the bridge too. Lorinda bought the house in the 60's for 25,000 dollars and it was now worth 200,000. However she still missed the prairie all the open space with no other people close by.

Upon arriving at Vanna's perfect brick and wood house and immaculate landscape, Lorinda realized there was an underground water system. Why hadn't she noticed it before? That's why everything was so lush and green. Although additions had been made to the house several times, they had kept the plantation type column at the front door and the huge down stairs windows with bay windows upstairs. The place looked like a picture from "House Beautiful". Vanna flew out the front door and gave Lorinda a big hug saying "You are so glamorous with your long curly black hair and your long skirt and everything matching right down to your shoes, Lord, who ever have thought a little tomboy like you would end up looking like a movie star." Lorinda stood shocked and said, "Thank you Vanna, no one has ever said that to me before! I try to dress and keep my hair up-to-date. I sell clothes, so it's necessary to look well good.

Lorinda thought to herself, "Vanna, only you could make me feel attractive again after a failed marriage and many bad relationships. I have little confidence in my appearance and my self-worth is at a low point right now.

Vanna took them through the sunlit rooms, yellow and blue furniture sitting on pale yellow rugs placed on gleaming wood floors and fireplaces glowing in each room. Floor to ceiling French doors led from the dining room to the huge covered patio with a brick fireplace and built-in-grill. The pool-size heated pond flowed up to the patio. The overwhelming sight of it all took Lorinda's breath away as she thought, just a little jealous, of her parent's small two-bedroom stucco house, small dark paneled rooms, few windows—cozy as it felt.

To the other side of the house sat a huge barn and countless out-buildings sitting almost to the edge of a bluff overlooking the badlands-like gullies below. All of the ranches here were built on the flat table land that resembled a picnic tabletop, then sloped down to the seat, then straight up and down rock, little grass tufts here and there, ending in the fertile valley below. Only cattle and sheep did good on the bare hills, the valley below was all farm ground.

Vanna served coffee and cream puffs, Lorinda's favorite. They talked nonstop until Lorinda noticed the sun going down. Before she left Vanna said "I'm calling everyone over Saturday night for a big wing ding. Dale can grill steaks and I think I will call Brian and Laura. Julie is home this weekend and I want her to see you. When we bought this place from Brian after mom and dad passed away, I never thought we wouldn't make it financially, but we made it with lots of hard, hard work and I love sharing our beautiful home with everyone. Well you might say I just love to have company."

CHAPTER 4

AFTER BLAKE GOT A call from Joel's mother, he started to think about all the things Joel had told him. Blake knew hardened criminals in his business as a counselor for inmates, but he also had a feeling when someone is being totally truthful. Joel seemed to be telling the truth, Blake had to trust his bull shit detector, that the prison guards insisted he was psychic he just seemed to know who would benefit from extra help returning to society or who was truly a bad ass all the way through, he felt from Joel's story, that Joel could not have set up an operation like he described without a lot of money and expert help to make crystal meth. Also he wondered about Joel's sentence, why such a short time for dealing and the witness's against him were the very same people he said was in on the deal.

Blake, now 27, graduated from college with a degree in social services and counseling. He went to work immediately with the prison system ending up at the Sioux Falls penitentiary for the last three years. He looked like an All-American tackle for a college football team-tall, blonde, and blue-eyed. He was from Iowa and moved to South Dakota to take a $50,000 a year job in the prison system. It was probably not the best job in the world, but he loved it. Blake was worried about Joel and started planning a trip to Northwest South Dakota, clear across the prairie state to the Black Hills. Yes, he would leave Saturday morning.

CHAPTER 5

JULIE DENNING WAS DRIVING home to Rapid City for the weekend. She was in her last year at South Dakota State University in Brookings, She missed her parents, Sheriff Brian Denning and his quiet stay-at-home wife, Laura. As Julie hurried to get ready for her trip, she looked at herself in the mirror and smiled at the beautiful blonde girl smiling back. She was tall with long blonde hair and looked like a model. Julie had, always wanted to be a nurse and was now close to accomplishing that goal. She couldn't wait to get home after leaving a three-year relationship with a young man at college, a man she realized that she did not know very well after all. Julie told her mother on the phone the night before that her former boyfriend seemed to be "shallow". She thought if mom and dad knew I caught him in bed with my room-mate, they would be more shocked than I am. She, for a few months had been carefully extracting herself from him, sensing he was a handsome man with no scruples, especially if he thought he could get by with something underhanded even cheating on tests. No, she would never tell her folks the truth about him, they liked him and was surprised when she said it was over.

Julie lived by Rapid City, her parents owned a huge house in the Black Hills between Middleborg and Rapid City, in Haines County where her dad was the Sheriff. She needed to see her loud, brassy "har, har" father and loving mother to get her feet on the ground again.

She had not a clue what a hornets' nest she was driving in to and she would be stung. Years later she could soothe her hurt by saying "In God's world something good always comes from something bad.

Laura Denning was an avid gardener and was getting ready for winter, a beautiful woman with few friends, she enjoyed her lovely home with hills covered with pine trees overlooking a canyon. Sometimes she felt guilty for having all the things she and Brian had acquired—an awe-inspiring home, new cars, and plenty of financial resources. Brian and his friends owned a luxurious guest ranch not far from their house as well.

Brian was a shrewd businessman in addition to his job as sheriff. He made wise investments after selling his parent's huge ranch to his sister, Vanna Schultz. He contributed to various charities, showed kindness and provided assistance to many young people, or anyone down on their luck. He personally drove prisoners in his private vehicle to the state penitentiary and to the juvenile prison, he called it quality time to visit one on one many a reformed prisoner had wrote to thank him.

Brian was gone most of the time, which suited Laura fine as she cared for her 12 room house and all her flowers, garden and ponds, occasionally with some assistance. Her daughter Julie was the light of her life. She knew Brian loved her—after his money and his job. Brian enjoyed being in control and hobnobbing with big shots like Judge Calder and States Attorney Fresman. They golfed and hunted together and were partners in many business ventures. Together they supplied the capital to buy up small companies, got them up and running and then let the original owners run them. Brian's motto, was, "It takes money to make money." Laura loved her husband, in an abstract way, in spite of their being opposites. He was a big handsome man who laughed easily, unless someone crossed him, then his blue eyes were like steel. His hair was peppered with distinguished grey at the temples. Everyone loved him.

Laura's dearest and only close friend was Nina Fresman, the States Attorney's wife. She supposed people thought they were "Mousey, brainwashed women" who stayed at home under their husbands' thumbs—and possibly this was true.

Judge Calder and his second wife, Megan, made up a threesome. Megan was 35 years old compared to his 50. Laura and Nina privately referred to Megan as the Judge's "bimbo" because she was so open and so obviously in love with money. One thing all three couples had in common was Julie; they were all like parents to her. The Calders and Fresmans never had a child of their own. Calder's first wife left and took his only daughter, who later died of leukemia. Maybe that's why he married Megan, who knows . . . . Nina and Doug Fresman never seemed to mind being childless. They traveled extensively every winter, spending two months or so at a friend's villa in Italy. The Calder's planned to go with them this year. Laura wondered how Nina could tolerate Megan for two months and desperately hoped Brian would never want to leave for the winter. Nina loved winter and Brian said, "They did not have that kind of money, yet." She wondered how the Judge and Doug had acquired so much.

CHAPTER 6

FRIDAY NIGHT MARGE MOSS worked late at the cafe. Sheriff Jim Ball came in looking worried. "Marge, I haven't heard a word about Joel or his car. It seems like he vanished off the face of the earth!" She said "I'm just worried sick, but I keep busy; it seems to help. I usually don't work nights, but I'm trying to make extra money in case I have to hire a private detective. I called that counselor from prison that Joel told me about; he's coming tomorrow. I don't know what to do . . . . Can you stay to eat?" Jim replied, "I guess I eat here nearly every night. I'm not much good at cooking since Mary died." Marge said, "I'm sorry. I know about, being alone since Al died, it's been so many years now that I'm pretty much used to it."

Sheriff Ball stayed and drank coffee and visited with others until Marge was off duty. He asked her if he could take her out for a drink at the local lounge. Marge was shocked; at 50 she had not been approached by any man for anything like a date. She said "I'd like to change clothes first. Stop at my house in about 15 minutes and I'll be ready."

As she drove home her heart was pounding as she thought "My son is gone and here I am excited over the sheriff being nice to me! Well I guess I'll live for the moment." She changed into a pair of Levi's and a bright western shirt with a silver conch belt and cowboy boots. She thought, "Why not? I was raised on a cattle ranch and rode a horse before I could walk." The clothes complemented her tall rangy body, long Miss Clairol hair, complete with blush and eye shadow.

Sheriff Jim drove up in his pickup. Marge grabbed her purse and hurried out to meet him. He exclaimed, "My gosh, you look different from when you were at the cafe." With a red face he said, "Well-Wow!" She laughed "Thanks, if anyone needs a night out it's me. This thing with Joel just has me crazy!"

All the other customers at the lounge started cat calling when they saw Jim and Marge walk in together. Everyone wanted to buy drinks for them, and there was lots of sympathy for Marge and worry over Joel, even though she could tell most thought he had just run off. Time flew by and it was closing time. Jim and Marge sat in his pickup outside her house and talked for an hour. He shyly asked if they could do this again sometime. She said, "Oh, I hoped you would say that; yes, yes, yes!"

As Marge got out of the pickup, she said, "There's one thing I would like to ask you. Joel told this Blake Denton, a prison counselor from Sioux Falls, the same story he told me and we both believe him. I'd like you to hear this story and see what you make of it. I figured you might be going out East to pheasant hunt, but if you aren't, could you come to my house about 2:00 tomorrow afternoon and meet Blake? I know you think Joel ran off." Jim grabbed her hand and said, "I will be there. My gut feeling tells me there's something fishy about all this." With tears in her eyes, Marge squeezed his hand. And as she walked toward the house she thought, "Thank you, God" over and over.

CHAPTER 7

SATURDAY MORNING LORINDA DID chores about 8:00 A.M. and after another huge Molly breakfast she said, "I'm going out and catch old Daisy, their twenty year old mare that Tom's kids, Lorinda and her Dad rode. Daisy, a gentle old horse came running up to the sound of sweet chopped grain in a pail. Red, Tom's horse was reluctant to come up, tail in the air off he ran, Lorinda put a halter on Daisy and thought, What the heck I'll try jumping on bareback, after two attempts she made it puffing she thought, your 47, what do you expect?

Daisy trotted to the barn, Lorinda holding on for dear life, disgusted with herself to be in such bad shape. She bridled and saddled, Daisy, then loaded up her sketch pad and a few paints in the saddle bags. Telling Molly she was going out to the break lands to try to paint the straight up and down cliffs, gullies and crevices. Friends in the eastern part of the state couldn't believe how flat some of the land is here until suddenly it drops off to the valleys below. She wanted to try painting especially the sky, and the various fall colors that the prairie produces. Molly called out "Watch for rattlesnakes this unseasonably warm weather, they will be out even though it is fall!

Lorinda stopped the horse and from the top of a hill she stood looking back at her parent's ranch, neat buildings, a steel shed, a barn and the white stucco house had one saving grace a wraparound porch on two sides of the small house, pretty pots of flowers, rocking chairs and a swing. There was no lawn, just scrubby weeds. Dad had painted all the buildings bright red except the house. The barn stood off to the right wooden corrals all around it, weathered gray, how she would like to paint them white, but she didn't dare mention that to her father, he would be insulted. The big old granary stood yet, she remembered the feel of scratch oats when as a kid she shoveled grain away from the elevator into the granary. All in all, though it was a nice place.

Daisy and Lorinda went about a mile on the flat land, at the top of the drop off, Lorinda put Daisy's reins down and then found a stick to poke around the flat rock she wanted to sit on—no rattlesnake, God, she hated any kind of snake, but even the thought of a rattler made her queasy. Sitting on the rock she felt instantly inspired to sketch out the scene and quickly mixed some colors trying to match the many shades of grass, rocks, yucca and sage.

Good Grief! With a great huff Daisy laid down on her feet, her head next to Lorinda's back. Lorinda laughing said "Don't you dare roll with that saddle on. Ah, Daisy, horses don't lay down like a cow!" So much for accurate sketching, Daisy kept rubbing her head on Lorinda's back. Happily she painted away using her bottled water to keep her acrylic paints from drying too fast. What a wonderful relaxing day. That's when the first helicopter flew over, Daisy didn't seem bothered by it, Lorinda decided it must be from the big air base located by Rapid City. When the second helicopter flew over breaking the golden silence, the horse did jump, then another huff and Daisy laid down flat like she was dead, at first Lorinda was alarmed and then she remembered what Daisy wanted, Lorinda laid her head down on the horse, put the painting aside, they both sighed with pleasure. She and the old horse had taken a few naps together over the years.

Suddenly Daisy jumped up knocking Lorinda aside, at first she thought "Snake", but the hair on the back of her head stood up someone was here or something, heart racing, she was instant mad, her peaceful morning was ruined, damn, damn. Casually looking around she saw a lone rider and horse about a mile to the west, with something shiny in the rider's hand, "Gun" then it dawned on her binoculars. Well, guess what, asshole. I have some with me too. She dug around in the saddle bags, until she found them then turned them toward the rider. The two of them were looking directly in each other's eyes; he just kept watching her, no one she knew of that she was sure. She put down the binoculars, thinking tough guy or mean looking, she wasn't going to hang around and find out. He and the stupid helicopters was ruining her day, really mad now she gathered up her stuff and headed for home, He was still standing in the same place watching her, but he never attempted to come any closer, not friendly like all the neighbors were in ranch country. When the third helicopter flew over, she was dumbfounded.

When Lorinda rode in the yard, Molly rushed out, "Are you all right? I tried your cell phone." Lorinda hit her head with her hand, "Oh, my God, I forgot it!! What the hell is with all the helicopters and some guy I never seen before, sat on a horse on the old Olson ranch land, watching me with "binoculars" what's going on around here?" Molly shook her head, "I know that's why I was worried about you, I have never seen that many helicopters in a week much less in a morning! What do you mean man on a horse? How do you know what he looked like?" Lorinda waving he arms "Because I had my binoculars with me and I looked him straight in the face, he was watching me for crying out loud! My peaceful morning shot to hell, plus I had to pee . . . I couldn't do it behind a bush with all the Looky Lou's flying around . . . . What. I'm a threat to Homeland Security or something?" It kind of freaked me out—ah scared or something!" Molly slapped her knee and laughed "This comes from a woman; who as a girl, loaded the shot gun-went to the corral—where her dad was trying to break up two bulls fighting. You marched up to a bull—face to face—and said, "Stop it right now before you hurt my dad or you are going to be one dead bull!!!" The bull ran off with his tail in the air." Mother and daughter both started laughing, Lorinda said," I guess should have said this morning made me mad; Not Scared!" The rider, well if that's the new guy, I kind of got a bad impression; He looked; what do I want to say? Sinister that's the right word." Molly went "Baloney, he's nice; maybe it was one of his hired men, they're kind of different."

"Oh, your Dad called, they're at the hunting lodge, they had steaks and some drinks last night. The Old Poop . . . . I hope he don't have a heart attack; he's not used to drinking that much and then the walking the fields, well I guess it's his life; right?" He said they did stop at Pierre yesterday and looked at the fighting Mustangs and World War II Memorials.

They all look so real, when we came to visit you last year, we went that way and looked at everything, with the lake and the ducks and geese all over, well, it was just beautiful. You should go home that way; it's worth the extra driving."

Lorinda curried Daisy and gave her a carrot and some forbidden sugar cubes, Daisy hung around the barn, like—hey—let's do this again, she did love sugar cubes.

Lorinda went to the house for lunch; chili and cornbread, she moaned "This is so good . . . . and you baked pies too??" Vanna called while you were gone and asked if I could bake a couple of pies, so I made an extra one for us, too. I guess she had some big party over there last weekend for a State Senator or somebody important like that, anyway she's all excited, she going to use the decorations and tablecloths from that party for tonight." Lorinda groaned "Is she going to all this trouble for me?" Molly snorted "More like, look how rich I am to all us poor neighbors, ha like we care." Aha, would you mind helping me in the garden this afternoon, with the squash and pumpkins, they didn't freeze yet and I can't get my old knee to bend like I think it should; darn body it's giving out on me?" Lorinda was shocked at her mother's huge garden; she thought how can she raise a garden like this in this dry land? Molly had a homemade water system running through the garden, holes cut in hoses that siphoned from a stock tank by the well that never seemed to run dry. As they worked together in the dirt, Lorinda admitted she only grew tomatoes, potatoes and cucumbers in her small plot at home. Molly said, "What about your beautiful yard full of flowers—that's your specialty—mine is vegetables?" Molly fussed that Lorinda was getting really dirty. She laughed then and said "You don't have to say it, Thank God, we finally got running water." "Mom, how did we do it back then, all the cooking, canning, cream cans to wash? How? "Well," Molly said, "One thing we know is we had the prettiest outdoor toilet in the country; remember the paint the lady in town gave you, our cream customer, a whole box of different colors, you went nuts, the toilet was every color in the rainbow, when you got done; you were so proud." Lorinda said, "Where is the old toilet?" "Out by the chicken house, your dad painted the outside red just this year, boy Oh, Lordy, the inside is still your doing." Lorinda thought back; fond memories of her beautification program for the ranch, like the star flower bed made from field rock, each rock painted a different color. Good memories.

CHAPTER 8

Marge Moss was so nervous she could not sit still, Saturday afternoon had finally came, she kept dusting, fluffing cushions, rearranging her angel collection. She had carefully dressed in black slacks with a white silky blouse and a simple gold chain around her neck. She wore small gold hoop earrings and with her hair swept up behind her head, making her look more refined—she hoped. Finally at exactly 2:00 Blake Denton and Sheriff Jim drove up at the same time.

She watched them from her front door. Jim was tall with black hair sprinkled with grey showing from under a cowboy hat, and a black handlebar moustache. Beside him was Blake, blonde, well built, dressed in pleated khaki slacks and a neat tan checked shirt. He had bright blue eyes, which made him look like the kind of intelligent "all American "boy" anyone could trust.

She breathed a sigh of relief and invited them in. They both noted her clean, attractive, simple home. She seated them at her antique oak table in the small dining room and poured coffee for them. They all relaxed as she got out the notes she had written to remind herself of everything Joel had told her.

In 2002 Joel had won a scholarship to Middleborg College, about 50 miles from Rapid City in Haines County. It is a small college with mostly medical and pharmacy students. Joel had worked in the local drugstore and hoped to be a pharmaceutical salesman. In 2003, over spring break, he had been approached by another student, Ted Heim, who asked if he would like to earn $10,000 for a weeks' work in a private lab. Heim said it was secret work and if he ever told anyone it would go bad for him. Joel thought about it over night and all he could think of was the money, even though he was sure it was illegal. The money won out.

He had recently told Marge how stupid he felt. They told him it was $15,000 for a week in the summer. The next day he accepted and by midnight, after final tests, he walked to the 7-Eleven Store and climbed into the back of an enclosed van that had its license plate covered with mud. He had called Marge and said he had a job grading papers for a professor over Spring break.

The van had a sliding wall separating the driver from the other seven boys who at different times climbed in with him. He thought they drove two or three hours. The van was backed up to a door in an underground building—cement block sides, eight beds and an enclosed perfect lab with all kinds of food in a deep freeze and a refrigerator full of drinks, pop, juice, milk—no alcohol,. Joel knew instantly from the ingredients, that he was making crystal meth, actually they were all having fun even though each one had a different excuse for doing this. Some said Well people are going to get meth where ever they can anyway, at least this won't kill them, it's made right.

On the third day someone opened the locked door and brought in Styrofoam boxes of hot food. That's when he took a chance and peeked out around a pipe that led to an anhydrous tank, at least that's what he was sure was next to the wall of the building. To his shock he saw a landmark a turtle-shaped hill. He refused to tell anyone why he recognized it. He thought of it as protection if he got caught. He knew that hill; his Dad took him hunting once for antelope and showed him the strange hill.

About midnight on the fifth night, after making what he guessed a million dollars worth of crystal meth, they were hurried into the same van and returned to the 7-Eleven.

Envelopes containing a wad of $100 bills for each were passed from the front of the van. When Joel got back to the dorm, he took out $1,000 and hid the rest above a ceiling panel in his bathroom. A few weeks later he went to a party and, after drinking a lot, he told the story. By afternoon the next day the Haines County Sheriff, a drug agent and the local police had a search warrant for his dormitory room. Of course, they quickly found the money, but to Joel's shock and outrage by now they also found a bag of crystal meth and said they had evidence he was selling it. Joel said over and over "I did not have meth in my room, it had to have been planted there!! He was handcuffed and taken off to jail. When Marge and his attorney got there to bail him out, he told them the whole story as well as the names of the boys he had been with. He insisted his mother and attorney tell no one about the turtle mountain. His attorney went right to the officers in; charge and each boy was questioned. They all said they were given a free vacation at a luxury guest ranch, and that they had been chosen because of their 4.0 grade average. They also said Joel was invited, but did not come. They had pictures and witnesses at the ranch where they spent Spring break.

Ted Heim came to visit him in jail and whispered, "You're a dead man if you don't plead guilty. The law will go easy on you. You should have kept your mouth shut. They have you for possession and selling, that's bad!" Joel did plead guilty and received what they said was a light sentence—six in the state penitentiary. In prison is where he started investigating on his own, whenever he was allowed computer time. He finally found out that the Haines County Sheriff Denning and Judge Calder owned the dude ranch where the other boys insisted they stayed. This he only told Blake and his mother and he talked about this turtle mountain, which nobody seemed to know about. He insisted that's how he would find this lab and prove that a lot of people were involved and get it shut down so no other young man was foolish enough to get involved, and have their life ruined too. Although the States Attorney from Haines County had told him, after probation and some community service, his record would be erased.

Marge went on "Only it has been two weeks now and it seemed to her as if Joel was gone forever. Finally she added that an attorney for a boy named Todd Ames kept calling for Joel. She gave the attorney's phone number to Jim and Blake.

Now Marge said "I'm sorry to be such a poor hostess, let me put some lunch I made earlier on the table and Blake tell us about your trip here and I guess you must have flew." He said "No, I left early this morning." "I really enjoyed the drive." Embarrassed she said "I'm sorry I didn't even introduce you to each other!" They both said they had introduced themselves outside and was as anxious to hear her story as she was to tell it. Marge felt like a weight had been lifted from her shoulders, to have a sympathetic car to listen to her for a change. She had told her father and sister all about Joel, but they told her to stop being so naive, Joel got what he deserved, think of all the young kids hooked on that awful drug. He was just darn lucky he didn't get 5 years in prison.

After lunch Jim and Blake both said they would do some checking around and see what come up. Also, Jim asked for a picture of Joel's "75 Nova." It should be pretty easy to spot because of its racing stripe down the middle. They both wondered why no one had seen the car.

After Blake left, Jim stayed a Marge's house for awhile. He asked, "If they could go out some place to eat this evening?"

She said "Please let me fix you supper, how about pork chops and a rented movie?" He said, "A home cooked meal sounds darn good. I'll do chores first." I should quit raising cattle, but I love living in the country and I need something to keep the grass down."

CHAPTER 9

When Blake Denton heard all Marge had to tell him, he asked for directions to Middleborg and then left.

He decided to interview a couple of the boys, if he could find them. By 6:00 P.M. he was at the college and lucky found Ted Heim and two other boys home, but ready to go out. They told him the same story, they were all at the guest ranch and could not understand why Joel would involve them—they were shocked at his awful slander.

Blake thought its daylight yet, I'll drive up to this guest ranch tonight it's still warm out and it was a beautiful drive through the Black Hills.

When he drove in, a lady was just getting in a car by the office. She came over to him and said "We are closed for the winter, but we do have cabins for snowmobiler's and we stable a few horses for the winter." He asked "Who would have been here last April?" "Oh, the Danfords run this place by themselves when there's just a few people staying." He said "What about spring break?" She said "They have a special week for the kids with the highest grades from Middleborg College . . . . You see the people who own this are on the board at the college . . . so they pick several students for a free week, Danford's take care of all that, I'm not here until May or June." Blake "Is it possible to meet the Danford's?" She said "I'll call them, they live right here in the caretakers house." Calling from a cell phone she told him they said to come right over, they live behind those pine trees to the right.

Blake was warmly welcomed into a lovely log home, by a kind old couple. He looked like an old time cowboy and she looked a sweet old Grandma. After homemade pie and coffee, he asked about last spring break, who all was here. When he had first arrived he had told them he was checking out a story, a Joel Moss had told him and that he was a prison counselor, that Joel was missing and he was looking for any little piece of evidence he could find regarding Joel and asked if Joel had ever contacted them. They said "No, but we were questioned before by the Sheriff, we are still puzzled why this Joel would make up such a story!" Dan Danford then got out their scrap book and showed Blake pictures of the seven boys Joel accused, and of all the other students they entertained last April.

Blake thanked them and then asked about their bosses. They said "They worked mostly for Sheriff Denning—there were others, but he wrote the checks. They both said what a good man he was and how he had invested in the stock market and made a mint. Blake drove off thinking, why in the world would Joel make up such a wild story unless some parts of it were true.

Blake rented a motel room in Rapid City, the closest big town, for the night. Before going out to eat he phoned the attorney, who had been calling Marge Moss. His name was Will States and he was representing a boy named Todd Ames. States on answering immediately invited Blake to his house close by, for supper. He insisted Joel come, he needed to talk and his wife loved company.

CHAPTER 10

MARGE MOSS MADE BANANA cream pie, set the table with her best china and went to the store for a video.

When Jim came back to a candlelight supper, he was amazed at all the baking. The house smelled wonderful. He said "I made some phone calls and put out a missing person memo for Joel and I faxed along a picture of his car, good grief, someone should have seen at least the car by now." Marge looked up at Jim shaking, tears dripping on her blouse, I know in my heart, right here, as she touched her chest; something terrible has happened to Joel: Oh, I know everyone says different but I know!" Jim went to hold her he thought "This funny lovely lady was right here under my nose all this time what's been the matter with me?"

He felt right at home at Marge's. Halfway through the movie he fell asleep only to wake up later, to find his head in Marge's lap and she was asleep sitting up with her hand on his head. He said "I have to go—this is crazy—I don't want to—ah, I like you so much!" She said "Same here as she kissed him good night." Jim told her he was on call for the weekend but he had his beeper and "Well what about tomorrow, what was she going to do?" She chuckled "I'm going to church and then I'm going to rake leaves and if you can think of something to get me out of that job, I'll jump at it, ha." "Well, could we eat out and then you come out to the ranch. I'll catch a couple of horses and I will show you my empire, well maybe just my small spread. She said "Pick me up at noon and I can't wait to see you again, if that sounds crazy I don't care!"

CHAPTER 11

LORINDA TOLD MOLLY "IT's getting late, Mom I enjoyed this afternoon so much, I can never go outside in town without neighbors either coming over or just plain watching me. This was fun, I'm going to go take a shower and wash my hair, I want to look special for Vanna's party tonight." Molly thought to herself, "Yeah, dear child but don't outshine Miss Vanna she might not be as nice as you think she is, if your competition for all the men's attention, her pretty blue eyes can turn to ice."

Lorinda came out dressed in a long black skirt with a black glittering top, with the back out. Molly gasped "That slit in your skirt is halfway up your ass! And here I'm wearing a plain long denim dress!" In the car Lorinda, hair swinging, all decked out down to black strapless spike heels, felt gorgeous, and looked gorgeous, probably because she was so rested up and relaxed. Molly quiet at first made a face. "I hope you're not after Don or Mike Pringle. I shouldn't say this but those two boys in their tight levis, fancy western shirts and coal black hair, remind me of mafia types on T.V. only in western clothing, there's something about those two that makes my skin crawl. Look at them careful, tonight, they act so polite, but I've heard some of the women they went with, different ones all the time, are afraid of them. So, now I've said my piece."

Lorinda shocked "I can't believe you said that, but for your information I watch them like a hawk. When I was a kid, Don hid by the barn, grabbed me, threw me down and was on top of me before I knew what happened. I put my knee in his crotch and used language, even you never heard. When I stomped off, I said I'll tell my Dad on you if you ever grab me again! I still laugh thinking about the look on his face! Honestly, they used to remind me of two tomcats circling around me. I'm a woman, so that's kind of flattering—except I don't ever want to be alone with either one of them. So there." She laughed.

Vanna had every light on in the house, she met them at the door in a shimmering white long gown, scoop neck, with what looked like a huge diamond necklace and long earrings to match. Her hair was styled like Lana Turner the movie star. She truly sparkled like a fairy princess. She took their jackets and said "I have the patio nice and warm." As they walked through the house to the dining room, that led to the patio, they saw Barney, their bow-legged old hired man, behind a portable bar. He was having the time of his life fixing drinks. The fireplace was on in the dining room, above it was a huge painting of horses and riders galloping along. Lorinda stopped and looked around at all Vanna's lovely china displayed in a huge oak china closet, besides two chairs in front of the fireplace and an oak dining set, nothing else was in the grand dining room, except two floor to ceiling fern like plants, that looked like trees. The entire east wall of the dining room was double French doors leading to the outside patio. When Lorinda walked out those doors she stood in awe, like a little girl in a toy store, everywhere there were miniature, clear lights, on all the plants and each table had a lace tablecloth, with the little lights draped around the lace skirts of the tables. On each table was an arrangement of yellow, blue and pink flowers, with white baby breath, tiny white flowers, here and there. The pillars of the patio had tieback curtains in a light shade of pink. Lorinda went to the curtains and was surprised, they could be drawn to enclose the whole patio, plus there was like a light weight mosquito netting behind the drapes so in the hot summer the drapes would be tied back, but the netting could be pulled to cover all sides of this beautiful outdoor room.

Vanna had candles big and small going everywhere, and of course her two chimeras—she used year round, always smoke going up, from her house.

Mike and Don Pringle rushed up to Lorinda to hug her and exclaimed how beautiful she was. They each had a young blonde bleached girl on their arm introducing them as their gals. Everyone said how good it was to see Lorinda, Why didn't she come home more often? Lorinda felt so happy to see her old friends. When Brian, Laura and Julie showed up there was a lot more hugging. Lorinda loved visiting with Laura about gardening and Julie was such a burst of fresh air, with funny stories to tell of her college days. Brian had always been the love of Lorinda's life, she compared every man she met with handsome debonair, Brian, the famous lawman. He was a charming man. Molly was standing talking to Dale Schultz as he grilled steaks, Lorinda really looked at her mother, good heavens she thought, Mom is a distinguished regal looking woman with her hair pulled back in a French knot and her unlined skin, why haven't I noticed this before, plus everyone seems to gravitate toward her, she is fun to visit with and so kind. When the Drakes arrived, the party was about to begin.

The new rancher was the last to arrive. He was a Burt Reynolds look alike, tall, dark, handsome even the funny laugh. Holy cow, Lorinda thought for once Mom was right, this guy looks good. Molly took him by the arm and brought him over to meet Lorinda. When she saw him up close, she did a double take, her unwanted lone rider from this morning. He took her hand and said "Ah, I believe we have a least seen each other before. I hope I didn't make you mad this morning. I just could not figure out what was going on! It's not often you see a horse laying out flat like it's dead and an attractive woman laying on its neck like she's dead!!" Shocked, Lorinda started to laugh, "Oh My God, I suppose Daisy and I did look dead, and yes, I felt foolish when I realized someone was watching! Turning to her Mother, "I guess Mom you might say we already have met, ah, binocular to binocular."

He said, "I kind of pictured you as some fancy lady from the big city; imagine my surprise when I found out you were doing chores for your Dad! I called the Drakes when I couldn't get your Mom on the phone, they told me all about you. Lorinda said, "I don't know what was worse you or the helicopters." Everyone started talking at once about all the noise. Dale said they even spooked his cattle!" The whole group started questioning if anyone knew what was going on. We never see that many that close together.

Molly said, "Lorinda, this is Burton Knight, Lorinda had to stifle a giggle, when he said "Call me Burt, your folks have been so good to me if I need help or advice, I head over to your Dad's and—well—the good cooking is regular drawing card too. Are you as good a cook as your mother?" Lorinda laughing, "No, I'm not quite as good, secretly I can't wait to get home for the cooking and the peace and quiet of the prairie." He said, "If the Air Force leaves you alone and (nosey neighbors). I did have to laugh when you and the horse jumped up, I sure am sorry I scared you!" Molly groaned and retold the story of Lorinda threatening to shoot a bull. The entire group laughed and laughed. Burt a little confused said, "What you're saying I'm lucky she didn't have a gun." Vanna took Burt's hand and led him off to meet the Dennings and others he had not met yet.

Dale called out, "Steaks are ready, some rare, some well cooked. He was a big man-tanned-healthy looking—with a snow white shirt and bolero tie, like a banker until you looked at his calloused hands.

Everyone gathered around, with their plates for steaks and baked potatoes, with all kinds of salads.

The Koi fish from the pond swam close to the patio for handouts of food, the scene was so peaceful and serene, Lorinda watched everything with sparkling eyes, what a magical night. As the evening cooled off Vanna pulled the curtains around the patio creating a warm comfortable, cozy feeling.

Lorinda sat by the Drake's catching up on their families, as the evening wore on she got to visit with everyone of her long time friends. She thought, Why don't I come home more often.

Vanna wanted Burt and Lorinda to see the new office they had fixed up. She led the way up the open stairway that overlooked most of the house. She said, "Lorinda, I couldn't help copying your white carpet from when we came to visit you, so I had it installed in the living room and up the stairs, because the bare wood was so-noisy-loud when you walked on it and I do love the luxury of thick white carpet, in fact, come, I had it put down throughout the entire upstairs, except the bathroom." Lorinda went "I'm afraid my white carpet looks pretty cheap compared to this, as she slipped off her spike heels) I got mine at a wholesale house that was going out of business in Sioux Falls. It's been down five years now and it still looks clean, I think." Burt said "You probably don't have children or much traffic, white, Lord it wouldn't last a day at my house!" Both Vanna and Lorinda laughed, "The neighbor kids about live at my place, because of the water gardens, they come to watch the fish, play in the water and are generally a pain in the butt, but I do love them." Vanna said "They call her the cookie lady." Burt went "AHA, so you are like your mother,"

As they started up the stairs Burt held out his hand to Lorinda, she surprised walked up the stairs holding his hand, it seemed so natural. At the top she clapped her hands to in delight; it was gorgeous gold metallic wall paper half way up the wall with gold gilded boards dividing the gold wallpaper from the stark white paint above. When they got to the office Burt exclaimed, "I'm not going to jump up and down like Lorinda, but I have to say this is exactly what I want, MY Goodness, I didn't expect to see this on a ranch.!" Vanna said "It keeps track of everything on the ranch, from expenses to cattle breeding, all our animals are registered, so it really helps, well we love it, I had the big window put in so it looks over the livestock and corrals."

Going back down the stairs, Lorinda and Burt were still complimenting Vanna. At the bottom of the stairs Lorinda leaned on Burt as she put her heels back on, she said, "I didn't want to break an ankle walking in all that thick carpet, wow, Vanna it's wonderful!" She stood up next to Burt and gasped "You're taller than me even in my heels, wow!" He laughed his goofy laugh, "You are a tall lady, I'll bet you don't meet many men, who stand above you with—what the hell are those shoes-? Spikes or what?" Lorinda turned and just caught a brief look on Vanna's face like ice were her eyes, Lorinda thought, "Holy Cow, she's jealous, for crying out loud, she has Dale, the most wonderful man in the world and she wants the new guy too!"

Several people were getting ready to leave so Burt and Lorinda joined Molly, who was cleaning up in the kitchen. Burt said "Is it true a sophisticated lady like you is the chore girl or are you just on vacation?" "Yes, I'm the city girl with a country heart and I'm damn good at chores . . . . Well the milk cow likes me anyway." He said, "What are you and your Mom doing tomorrow? I'd like to take the two of you out to dinner." Lorinda was breathless for a minute, "You bet, she said, "How about after church at Placerville, Al's Place, the food is wonderful!"

Everyone as saying goodbye and leaving Lorinda and Burt stood visiting with the Dennings, while they were leaving, Brian, Laura and Julie all said what a treat it was to see Lorinda and meet Burt. Brian told him he was born and raised on this ranch.

Brian started out the door and then turned back "Vanna I'm going to take a couple of prisoners Monday morning to the Sioux Falls penitentiary, how about your special caramel rolls and hot coffee? It will be a nice break for them and me." She said, "Sure, and stop at that big grocery store, I'll call in an order.""Oh! He groaned—"I guess I can." Then Vanna said "Julie, are you going home Sunday?" "No, Monday morning." Vanna, "Oh please stop on your way or caramel rolls too." Julie said, "Oh, boy I wouldn't miss that—it's a nice break for me too."

Burt carried Molly's pie dishes to their car and told her, he was taking them out for dinner. Molly shook his hand and told him "Anybody asks me out to eat is the best in my book."

Driving home Lorinda sighed, "Mom, I really, really like that Burt, he's not only good looking, he's just plain nice, except for one little instance, I don't think he likes Vanna, when her back was turned, I saw him looking at her, well I know this sounds dumb, but like he hated her. Molly surprised, "Well she does come on to men kind of strong, maybe he thinks she's after him." Lorinda snorted, "Comes on to them, My God, if looks would kill, I'd be dead, she didn't like me leaning on Burt to put on my shoes, like she was jealous, maybe I was getting a little too friendly myself, I don't know!"

Molly said, "Honey you were just your usual happy go-lucky self and that's what I wanted. I knew he was perfect for you. He retired from some big important job in Texas, something to do with civil service and he is divorced, plus he has two kids that are married, they were here this summer." Lorinda went, "Yeah, Mom, but you know my bad luck when it comes to men, I can catch them like flies to honey, after a few times of dating I want to swat them too." They both laughed and then wistfully, "I bet there's many a woman who would give her eye teeth to find a catch like him, so I am going to think (Live for the Moment) have fun, go home, forget about it. I won't forget what a good time I had tonight, Imagine Vanna jealous of me!"

Molly said "How often do Vanna and Dale come to your house?" "Oh, about once a year or so, they deliver bulls to some farmer by Sioux Falls and they stay about a day, we go out to eat and I have them over for breakfast, sometimes if it's on a weekend. They never stay overnight with me, but we sure enjoy visiting the short time they're, there." "Oh, I forgot, last year Brian and Vanna came, she rode with him while he transported a prisoner to the penitentiary, we just had a blast, going from lounge to lounge, having a few drinks and visiting with all kinds of people. "Well anyway," Molly said, "I admit I would like you closer to home."

CHAPTER 12

BLAKE DENTON FOLLOWED WILL States directions to his house. He guessed they were a young couple by all the kids' toys in the driveway and garage. It was a very nice, new brick home, in an obviously new neighborhood, all young trees and lots of kids playing, outside. He was warmly welcomed by a tall thin, young man, who looked like exactly what he was; an attorney. He looked just plain nice and so did his tall blonde beauty of a wife, she was quick to shake his hand, invite him in, saying, we both work in the office even on Saturday, if we need to. I'm a paralegal and his gopher, digging out all the facts and yes, I bring him his coffee. Beth and Will States and forgive any mess, the kids have been busy tearing up the house. Blake put down his briefcase and looked at their lovely home overlooking a golf course, he whistled, "There's more money in Lawyer work than I make, I can see that." They relaxed outside on the deck, with drinks while Beth put supper on the table, takeout food from the local seafood place, it was delicious. After supper Will and Blake went to Will's Den. He explained, "It was the only room off limits to the kids." Blake had enjoyed playing a game of old maid cards with a five and seven year old after they ate. Both were exceptional, smart little boys.

Will said, "Actually Beth knows more about this case than I do, she did all the research, so when she gets the children settled, we will hear what she found out, as for me, "I'm determined to check this secret lab story out. It's hard for me to believe two young men have the same story and got almost the same sentence, even though Joel was accused of selling meth. Todd went to the authorities on his own, thinking he would get a better deal and he felt a responsibility for his stupid actions. When he turned himself in, they ran him through the court system so fast I couldn't keep up with just the evidence alone much less interviewing all the people involved. Todd Ames has to go to the Sioux Falls penitentiary, Monday, for six months. I promised him and his parents I would get to the bottom of this.

Beth came in, sat down with a wine glass in her hand, Will got up to get Blake and him a mixed drink. Beth picked up a file and started going through it for her notes. She said, "I left a cell phone number on the bulletin board at the college cafeteria in Middleborg, late one night, I got a call from a young woman, I think; to check with a Joel Moss from Willis, ask him how he got railroaded just like Todd, and hung up. Well I tried the Moss home and his mother explained he had come up missing and you were coming to help her try to find out what happened to him. I decided right then we needed to talk to you." Blake told her everything he had heard at Marge Moss's and said, "I think a local sheriff from Joel's home county is starting to get interested in this case. "Well", Beth said, "I got very little help from the Haines County Sheriff or the States Attorney there; to me they seemed like—well, a good old boy group-who thought women should stay home. What I did find was a D.C.F. corporation that seems to own millions of dollars in property, but I could not find the real owners names, only the people who sold the companies to D.C.F. and then ran them for the corporation. That so called guest ranch was one property by this corporation and it seemed to play a big part in both Todd and Joel's testimonies.

Also, the couple supposedly running the guest ranch have been the, main witnesses, stating that the other young people Todd told us about were staying at the guest ranch. Well guess what they signed their statements Dan and Alma Danford, but I cannot find those names in any system. What I did find was a Dan and Alma Ford who own property in Arizona." Blake told her he had been to the Danford's that afternoon and they seemed sincere about what they knew." Will, stepped in with the fact that Beth had tried the D.E.A. the F.B.I. and the local C.I.D. Beth angry said, "It was like talking to a brick wall a lot of hee-hawing around but nothing helpful." Will went on to say, "My best guess is all these law enforcement departments are somehow involved and we are messing up their investigation." Blake put his hand on his head and said "I am going to try to meet with this sheriff, district attorney or whatever he is, and anyone else he could find to answer some questions and then he told them about this Turtle Mountain that Joel was so determined to find." Will thoughtful, "Maybe call the federal people about that and ah, don't tell this bunch of good old boys, perhaps they have something to do with this or better yet are protecting someone who does know all about it, who the hell knows, this has been the strangest case, I don't know who to trust."

Driving back to his motel room, Blake was running all this information through his mind. He thought I'm more confused than ever, there is, something wrong here, In his room he started pacing the floor. He stopped and remembered hearing one of his former classmates in college was now an F.B.I. agent in Minneapolis, Minnesota, yes, Bob Allard. Would he dare call him this late at night? He always had his address book with him, yes, so what the guy could always tell him to go to hell! Bob Allard answered with a very sleepy voice, confused as to who Blake was. He said, "Oh, I remember you, ah this is kind of strange, ah, how are you?" Blake started talking as fast as he could explaining why he was calling and that for some reason no one seemed to know about this Turtle Mountain." Blake could tell by now, he had Bob's complete attention.

Bob Allard awake now said, "Denton, you have given me the missing puzzle piece to a dramatic scene no one has been able to find, I don't know how to thank you and never, ever worry about calling me in the middle of the night with important information like this!" Blake said, "I'm guessing you're not going to tell me what's going on." "No," give me your number where I can get a hold of you, honest I will explain everything to you when I can." They talked a few more minutes and he could tell Bob wanted him to hang up. Blake still could not sleep so he called Will and Beth States, who were as puzzled as Blake and asked him to call them when and if Bob ever told him anything.

Blake Denton had not a clue that his little puzzle piece would destroy a whole lot of lives, but a whole lot more lives would be saved because of it.

SUNDAY MORNING

Blake got up about 8:00 and started thinking about all the conversations he had during the last two days. He decided to try the sheriff's office and see if he could get an appointment to meet with Sheriff Denning on Monday morning. The dispatcher answered, Blake explained who he was and that he was here on a mini vacation, plus he wanted to find a Joel Moss who had been at the penitentiary and now seemed to have disappeared off the face of the earth. The dispatcher said, "Sheriff Denning will be gone on Monday, he is driving a prisoner to Sioux Falls, you can visit with him there or I can call him and see if he wants to see you today, he is very concerned about Joel Moss." Blake, "Yes, I certainly would like to see him today; if at all possible, I will leave my cell number with you.

To Blake's surprise his phone rang within five minutes it was Denning and he said "I think I know who you are, I believe we have met once or twice at the pen." Blake answered, "I think I remember you too, but I meet so many people I'm not sure." Denning said "Tell you what I'm grilling salmon steaks for lunch today, District Attorney, Doug Fresman, and Judge Calder are coming over to my house. Why don't you come too about 12:00? We have church this morning and it's such a nice day I thought let's have lunch outside, I'll give you directions to my house, call this number if you get lost. We are all concerned about Joel, we are all on the board of the college he goes to. He is such a good student and very well liked I have asked a few of his friends if they have seen him, nobody seems to know what the world could have happened to him, they all pretty much think he ran away." Blake said, "That's pretty much what everyone thinks I just kind of want to help his poor mother by checking out everything I can as to where he might have got off too, and I would love to come for a grilled salmon, I gather you're a fisherman?" "You bet," and I caught the fish in the backwoods of Washington State, that we're going to eat. We'll see you about noon."

Blake cell phone rang again after he hung up from the sheriff, it was Will Sates, "Blake, do you want to go to church with us, the kids would love it they took quite a shine to you. I thought we could go to eat afterwards." Blake told him about the invitation to the Sheriffs, but he would go to church with the States." Will went, "Ah, Blake, Beth and I were talking about your late night phone call and, ah, well we don't think you should tell anyone about it yet and maybe it's none of my business, but I don't know why . . . . I don't think you should mention this Turtle Mountain to anyone else." Blake interrupted with, "I have the same feeling, this old couple at the guest ranch using a different name, kind of bothers me. This Denning sounds like he is really concerned about Joel and I guess I have met him before, he seems like a really nice guy, oh . . . by the way this attorney Fresman and this Judge Calder are coming to the sheriffs for lunch too . . . I think I'll just ask a few questions, but not give any information other than what they know I already know." I'll see you in about an hour." Will jumped in with, "Don't worry about a suit, our church is pretty casual. Blake laughed, "I already got my best bib and tucker on, I kind of wanted to look professional if I had to go over to the Haines County sheriffs office."

CHAPTER 13

SUNDAY MORNING BROUGHT ANOTHER beautiful fall day. Lorinda hurried to do chores everything went along fine, she sighed, I think I'm getting kind of a routine going, not quite as so chaotic as the first couple of days. When she went to the house Molly had a mouth watering breakfast all ready. Lorinda said over her shoulder, heading for the shower, "How did I used to get the milk cow smell off me when I was a kid or the manure smell!" Molly, "Well I guess everyone smelled the same back in those days, a once a week bath had to do." "What, ah, are you wearing for this occasion?" Lorinda, mischief in her eyes, "Well what's wrong with what I wore last night? At Molly's shocked look, she said "Ma, I did bring along a conservative, white jacket and white blouse to go with a bright pink flowered skirt, Ha "When Lorinda come out in her pretty outfit, Molly smiled, "You have good taste in clothes, where you got that from I don't know because I pretty much wore simple plain Jane stuff." "Grandma, O'Malley, I'm sure she never did a days' hard work at least not in the field or chasing cows or butchering chickens. She was kind of a prima donna, when I was growing up, but she did love nice things. Remember when she got after me for saying "bull" she said it's a gentlemen cow, my dear. Good grief, she worried a lot about my skin, so I wouldn't be tan and coarse looking. Now being tan is the in thing. What she did teach me was to love art and reading, but she also helped me with the very worst fault and that's my constant wanting champagne on a beer budget, not all her fault, but I have always lived way beyond my means, I love to shop and I adore beautiful clothes, dishes, furniture, paintings, you name it and I think I have to have it!!" "They both laughed and Molly said, "Prima Donna, huh, I never thought you knew that." When they got in the fancy car for church, Lorinda looked at Molly she said, "This car is a luxury, that I cannot afford, but I would personally kill anyone that tried to take it away from me, I love it so and that's just plain stupid. I have to work extra to pay for it."

The church was packed; Molly made her way to the front, Lorinda groaned to herself, boy, she wants everyone to know I'm here, Holy cow, at home I sit in the back row.

It was wonderful seeing everyone again, as they stood outside visiting after church. A lot of hugs and remember this and that went on from Lorinda's childhood friends. Pictures of grandchildren and children got passed all around. Burt Knight was visiting with several of the other ranchers, but kept looking toward Molly and Lorinda. As they were finally walking to the car, he caught up with them, "I'll pick you two lovely ladies up in an hour." Lorinda blurted out, "Wow, you look so suave and dignified in your suit; should we dress up for dinner?" He said "You're not dressed up?? You look fancy to me, I'm taking you to AL'S, please lets all go casual. I'm tired of this suit already, I wore one for twenty five years on my job and I don't miss it!" Lorinda asked, "What was your job?" He said, "I was civil service, ah, kind of an inspector for the government mostly based in Texas, but I traveled all over . . . . Too much I guess, because years ago, my wife left taking our two children with her. My grown kids love to come out her to the ranch, so I didn't lose them completely. I was born and raised on a Texas ranch, we had hard times and my folks lost the ranch it about killed my Dad, but they live in town now and he fix's things for the whole town, actually he says he makes more money now then when he was on the ranch. My folks come and stay in the summer, but they don't like the winter here."

Lorinda and Molly hurried home to change. Molly said "Wear that nice levi set with the pink sweater, you look so pretty in that and wear your cowboy boots." Lorinda laughed, "Mom, you are trying to fix me up—forget it—I'm too old to fall in love again and did you notice every single woman in church eyeing Mr. Burt—I don't stand a chance, but you know my motto "Live for the moment", we'll just have fun for today, Okay?'

Burt drove up in a fancy black SUV. Lorinda said." Wowser . . . . you found out about gumbo mud here; didn't you? I'll bet this thing will walk right through it." He laughed (his hearty laugh) made her smile. "Yep", he said, "And talking about vehicles, what about that classy little job your driving? What is that some kind of sports car? It sure looks expensive." Molly snorted, "Her Grandma made her buy it!" Lorinda went in to peals of laughter at the puzzled look on Burt face, "Your Grandma's alive I guess I have not met her." Molly said, "She has been dead for years, she was a grand old girl and apparently, from what I learned this morning had a big influence on my two young children, as to wanting the finer things of life. (Spend Today you Might Be gone tomorrow, Worry about Paying it next year!) That's how she lived her life and Lorinda tells me she has to work extra hours to pay for all her dreams, Well Hell, that not's going to hurt her I guess, as long as she don't go completely nuts with this "I have to have it, because Grandma says (Live It Up),Ha!" Burt, "Well Lorinda I spend way more than I can make right now trying to get this ranch off the ground, I can't blame Grandma, but I can blame my need to have things, on being dirt poor as a kid and I worry if I think I'm going to lose something."

Burt carefully helped Molly in the front seat of his SUV, Lorinda in the back, thinking "HE Is a Nice Man". They talked about their lives and their families all the way to the restaurant.

At AL's buffet they met the Pringles and the Schultz's, both Mike and Don looked almost mad. They said, "We were going to call you to meet us, Lorinda!" Burt ever diplomatic, "Well let's all sit together." The conversations flowed with things from the past and present each talking about what they're doing now. Mike and Don talked about the summer rodeo's and they were going to Las Vegas for the championship with their horse and roping steers plus selling saddles and bridles they made last winter. Molly and Burt kind of sat back and enjoyed all there remember when's. Lorinda told stories about her customers, her house, and of course, all about her son Seth and Amanda, and how excited she was to be a Grandma. It was a wonderful time for everyone, so Lorinda thought, she felt so happy and relaxed and Burt putting his arm around the back of her chair made her day, it felt so good to have a man be with, well, be with her, so many events she went to alone and tried not to be jealous of the women who had husbands, or some man sit with them.

Driving them home Burt said, "I really needed this day just to get away and do something with people instead of, well, cows." The three of them chattered all the way to Molly's. Molly said, "You're coming in Burt for a special piece of pie I saved for you. Take it home if you can't eat it now. Lorinda will eat it all if you don't." She put it on a dish for him. He had to leave to check some fence. As he was leaving "Ah, Lorinda, could I take you out tonight to a movie in Rapid City; Molly you come too." "No," Molly said, "You two go." Lorinda said "I would love to go to a movie, what time?" Burt told her "Oh, let's eat out again, so I am thinking would 5:30 be too early?" Lorinda said "I'll be ready." Molly looked at her, "Me thinks you might be missing city life just a little bit, huh,.."

When he was gone Lorinda threw her arms around Molly, "Mom he IS something. I haven't been this excited about going out for; well years." Molly a funny look on her face, "Lorinda, I kind of paid attention to Burt and the look on his face, when he looked at Vanna was, . . . I guess your right HE really don't like her! I was shocked and when those silly Pringles boys were bragging up a storm to you, I seen that look you talk about."

Lorinda frowning, "Mom, when we were waiting for you by the car, Burt asked me if the Pringle's ever came to Sioux Falls to see me, he took me by surprise, I said, "No", but Vanna and Dale come sometimes twice a year. It seems funny to me that you asked me the very same thing. Did he ever ask you?" Molly said, "Yes, indeed he did, I wonder why he so curious about you . . . . or maybe them. Maybe he's jealous, that seems dumb though because you just met."

Lorinda musing, "I'm not very lucky with men they all in the long run turn out to be stinker's . . . I guess I'm looking for something to be wrong about him so I won't be hurt if he ends up not liking me. Mom is he, ah, is he a Christian or is the church just a social club that he thinks is necessary to be accepted in a new neighborhood? Better yet, does he believe in God?" "He told your Dad and I that when he was young he felt Jesus saved one of his children from some mysterious illness and after that he believes in an all powerful God that lets us make mistakes, but then helps us straighten them out, like a real Dad, only far more powerful." Lorinda thought fully "What a relief if you saw "The Look" then I don't have to explain what I mean. My guess is he is all man. I watched him too; his eyes were kind of hooded like a clever hawk, watching even me when he thought I wasn't looking. Well I'm going to . . . ." Molly laughed, "Live for the moment, and your right, furthermore, I don't think I have ever enjoyed you as much as this visit. Don't get me wrong I love you more than myself, but you used to be . . .

ah . . . kind of a smart alec, just sometimes, like I should do all kinds of things different. You didn't really say anything I could . . . well . . . feel it." Lorinda was shocked, "I love you Mom, IN—fact I worship you and when I grow up I'm going to be a fine dignified lady like you!"

CHAPTER 14

SUNDAY MORNING

Blake Denton met the States family at their very modern, new Church. He really enjoyed coffee afterwards with other young attorneys, friends of Will and Beth's. They did not talk about the case, but rather the sights Blake should see before he left for home and they were all interested in his job.

Blake left after giving the States children a big hug and promising to keep in touch with Will and Beth. Blake carefully read the directions to the Denning home. After driving for 30 minutes up and down hills he spotted their street sign.

When he found the right mailbox, he followed a driveway to a beautiful house, all brick, a landscaped yard with retaining walls all down the hillside-with bushes and fall flowers still blooming. The forest surrounded the property on all sides with the house and garage sitting like in a cleared acre or so. He thought God, this is like paradise.

When Blake rang the doorbell a beautiful blonde girl came to the door, "Can I help you." Blake said, "If this is the Sheriff's house—I think I was invited for lunch." Julie Denning looked shocked, "Holy Cow, I thought you would be some old man!" She put her hand over her mouth. "Well I guess I spoke first; thought last—please come in." She led him through the gorgeous house, one whole wall was huge windows overlooking more terraced beds of flowers, done with natural rock. Steps and paths wound down a hill to a babbling creek below. They went through French doors to a huge deck, with a roof, a hot tub and pool below the deck. Beyond that a glass green house with bright flowers blooming like summer only they were inside. Sheriff Brian warmly shook his hand introducing him to Laura, Doug and Nina Fresman, Judge Calder and Megan. He said, "And of course you have already met our daughter Julie, she goes to college in Brookings, South Dakota, close to your neck of the woods." Blake felt welcome immediately and thought well, they're really nice people, but wow, sophisticated and very intelligent looking. Laura was beautiful with blonde hair framing her lovely face. Nina was dark with long black hair, vivacious would describe her. Doug, the Judge and Brian were all tall handsome men dressed in casual clothes that cost more than his best suit, thought Blake. Megan looked like a bombshell all sleek and slinky like a model or something. She seemed to be nice and she held the Judge's hand like she held on for dear life. Blake tried to look interested in everyone there . . . it was hard for him to take his eyes or his mind off Julie; even her laugh was like a melody.

Julie sat next to him at the table, on the deck. There was good conversation over the grilled salmon steaks. They all seemed to be interested in Blake's work and asked a lot of questions, he in turn asked each of them about their work. Laura asked him what brought him out west. Joel explained that he had . . . had a model prisoner in Sioux Falls. This boy got out on parole and just disappeared. Blake said, "He had met this boys' mother when she came to visit him and she had called Blake to see if he could come for the weekend and give her some advice as to how to go about finding him. Blake told them he had visited some of Joel's friends at the college and also visited some of the witnesses that testified against him. He went on to say that on Saturday he had visited a beautiful guest ranch where two of the witnesses lived, it was an awesome place and the old couple running it were just so nice. Julie clapped her hands, "Guess what, Blake everyone at this table worked for three summers fixing up that ranch, all of us own it together, I personally varnished every log in that whole place. Mom and Nina scrubbed up those old cabins and the guys here did all the outside of the buildings and cleaned out years of muck from the stables!" Megan, looking at her long fingernails, pouting, and what did I do?" "Oh, Julie said, "You got all the business part done, she sat up the computer system and the reservation web site plus lots of advertising, sorry Megan, without her Joel we still would be just a local dude ranch, now we get people from all over the world." Blake told them he was impressed and would love to stay there some time. He asked, "What made you buy a guest ranch or how did you find it?" Brian spoke up, "Well my folks passed away and my sister Vanna bought my share of the ranch they owned. I was afraid of the shaky stock market, then I ran across this rundown dude ranch . . . . so looking at all the others . . . I kind of drug everyone in on making it profitable and believe me it has turned into a little gold mine." Everyone started talking about really how much fun it had been. Brian said, "After lunch the three of us involved in Blake's young man's case, one Joel Moss, will go over the paper work we have on him."

True to his word, right after lunch, Brian invited Blake, the Judge and the States Attorney to his den, where they each found big comfortable chairs bookcases covered the walls and a huge fireplace that was obviously used on a regular basis, made of natural rock covered most of one wall. Brian brought a lot of paperwork out of a briefcase by his desk and explained it was a little irregular to show a private person all the investigation notes, but since Blake was in the same business, namely law enforcement, Brian felt there was nothing illegal about letting Blake read everything. He had made copies and handed them out. All of the three older men lit a cigar, the den came complete with it's own ventilation system. Brian explained none of them drank, so no brandy with the cigars. Blake laughed, "I'd be afraid to drive if you all knew I was drinking!" They all kindly told him they remembered Joel and had tried to help him to no avail. They checked out his testimony and it all turned out to be lies.

After hashing over the case for some time, Blake reluctant said, "I had better move on or I'll miss seeing at least some of the Black Hills. He thanked them and shook hands with each man and commented on how thorough they had been trying to dig up facts, to help out a young man, who possibly didn't deserve it. The women were sitting outside commenting on the almost hot fall day. He thanked Laura and told Julie, Nina, and Megan, he was glad to meet such a nice bunch of people. Julie and Laura said, "Oh, we were going to show you the yard!" Blake said, "I would like that, I do want to see Mt. Rushmore before I go back, but there's still time." Julie walked beside him telling him about her intern nursing job and college. He could hardly talk she looked like a movie star—only—inside a very down to earth girl. After looking at the yard and greenhouse; he said, "Thank you again, I'd better go." Julie said, "Would you like me to go with you? I'll be your tourist guide." Blake a huge smile on his face, "Oh, would you I would really, really like that.?"

She said, "We'll take my car; okay?" Off they went in her little red sport car. He relaxed after awhile and talked about his growing up years. He had five sisters, so he told her tales of being the only boy, in a big happy family.

As they climbed up the steps to Mount Rushmore, he held her hand and said in awe, "It is more spectacular than I thought!" They stopped to rest by an enclosed clump of pine trees, the breeze seemed to whistle a song through the trees to them. Blake said, "I feel so peaceful, thank you Julie, I needed this." They drove all over the hills then, it was time for supper at a local truck stop; where Julie said the food was wonderful and it was. Julie then said, "Do you want to go to a movie? It's too late for you to drive back tonight. Can you take a day off tomorrow? I don't have to go back to school until Tuesday, then we could follow each other back east and stop at my Aunt Vanna's for breakfast on a real cattle ranch by the badlands. Can you stay at your motel one more night or would you want to stay at my folks; there's plenty of room?" "Oh no," Blake said, "I can't stay at your folks, I already have my room for another night, I didn't dream I would get to see your Dad today so I planned on staying until Monday anyway. I would love to go to a movie and could we get my car, so I can drive out of your mountain country in daylight, I'm not as good as you with these winding curves and ah, well the straight down view from the road is nice, but I sure as hell wouldn't want to make a mistake and drive off the edge."

When they got to Julie's house; she ran in to tell her folks she was going to a movie with Blake. Blake followed her little red car down the hill toward town, they left his car at the motel and then Julie whipped all over town showing him the sights before the movie.

Brian Denning fuming to Laura, "What the hell is she doing, we have hardly seen her? I REALLY DON'T LIKE THIS GUY, WHOEVER HE IS . . . SNIFFING AROUND HER!" Laura laughed, "I think he's nice . . . your just jealous." "Whatever! I'm going to check him out anyway.

CHAPTER 15

SUNDAY AFTERNOON

Jim Ball drove up to Marge Moss's exactly at noon, he found her out back raking leaves. She was surprised to see him. He apologized for not calling first, but he couldn't get her on the phone. He said, "Let's go out to eat, and then 'ah' I'd like you to come out to my place and go horseback riding. Don't change clothes, you look fine to me." Marge had to laugh, "I'm glad I look fine to you, but I'm going to change and fix my hair anyway. Come on in have some coffee while I get ready and you bet-I love to ride, I'm sure you know I go out to my brothers and help with the cattle summer and winter." "No." Jim said, "I didn't know that until this morning when I had coffee uptown, the guys told me."

Marge hurried to get dressed in Levis and a jacket and her favorite boots.

Jim was obviously proud of his ranch as he showed her the house and then out to the corrals where he had a couple of horses inside the barn. He told her all about each horse, when they were born and how old they were. They rode out along a now dry creek bed, with lots of willow trees and brush covering it. Marge leaned back in her saddle and looked at the perfect sky, one or two lazy fluffy clouds floating over a bright blue she thought what a perfect day. Jim said, "I can't ride out too far I'm on call, my beeper and my cell phone keep me connected, but if something happened I have to drive to town right away." Marge said, "It's been a wonderful two or three days and what were you doing talking about me to the guys in town?" Jim blushed, "Are you mad, I'm sorry, ah . . . I wanted to know more about you . . . I'm sorry." Marge went into peals of laughter "Silly man, I don't care I'm teasing,. What did they say" Old Marge is quite a gal but don't piss her off, she will tell you in no uncertain terms if she thinks you're out of line."

Jim's face turned red again, "How did you know that's what they said?" "Because I watch those good old boys so they don't try anything funny like pinching me in the ass or using dirty language when I'm serving them their lunch. They seem to respect me and I try to keep it that way." "Marge threw back her head and said I'll race you back to the ranch." Galloping along for all her horse was worth she beat Jim by a head. They both took saddles off and curried their horses. A loud beeping sound came from Jim's crotch embarrassed he hunted around for his beeper. "Muttering he said, "The damn thing must have fell off my belt." He called in on his cell phone, a strange look come over his face.

"Marge, I think we had better go into the office for this message. The dispatcher just got a fax in from the Sheriffs' office in Durant County that's south and east of here, it seems . . . . now just maybe . . . a guy called in about seeing Joel's car and just heard he was missing."

Marge was in Jim's pickup before he could say another word. She had her hands in a praying position when he got in. She said "I'm sure Joel is dead I don't know how I know, but he is . . . dead. I just want so bad to know what happened to him and why!"

When they got to the office, the dispatcher gave him the sheriff's cell phone number from Durant County, he said to call anytime, that he is going to check this tip out on Monday or better yet you could come out here and interview this witness. I'll tell you what he told me. His name is Alfred Tate, he runs AL's Diner and gas station by a little town called Placerville, it's about fifty miles from Rapid City, east and he don't remember exactly the date, but sometime in the last two weeks, a kid matching Joel's description-well he said he remembered the old classic car with the racing stripe first—then realized that's the kid they're hunting. This kid wanted to know if Al knew of a turtle shaped mountain or hill. "Sure," Al said, "You can only see old turtle hill in the spring and fall; when the grass is short. The hill is perfect round, with rows of grass and little scrub bushes making it look like scales on a turtle's back. A smaller hill in front has bushes, or like small trees growing straight out. The feet are piles of rock on the sides—actually the trees have an open place in the middle of the neck that looks like an eye. This kid asked "Where he could see it the closest?" Al told him there's several ranches around it, he gave the boy their names. Al told him, "Look, I'll call a couple of them so you can drive up to it on their land." While he was still on the telephone, he turned around and the kid was driving off! "Jim went to his computer and looked up the area, it didn't mention a turtle hill, but he did get the names of the ranchers in the area, close by the road going North of Placerville. He had thanked the Durant County sheriff over and over for the help. Jim decided to try calling some of the names, but no answers except one and they had never seen Joel or his car.

All this time Marge sat on a folding chair not moving with her hands over her eyes. Jim went to her and gently pulled her hands away, "Honey, we will find your Joel one way or another. Do you think you could take tomorrow off work? I have the day off, let's just drive down there and visit AL's Diner and some of those ranches, you up for that??" Marge started jumping around flopping her hands above her head; laughing with tears running down her face." Jim horrified stood shocked shaking his head. "Oh, Jim don't worry this is what I call my snoopy dog dance, if I could flop my ears I would, Oh God, I won't be happy again until I know where Joel is but this is a start and the most information I have eeceived since Joel came home that day. My family has been embarrassed by the whole mess, so they have been absolutely no help." She threw her arms around Jim and gave him a kiss. The dispatcher started giggling, covering her mouth, big tough Jim looked like a lovesick teenager, holding Mrs. Moss in his arms. He gave the young dispatcher a stern look and led Marge out of the office to his pickup. He said, "Stay with me tonight . . . . Ah . . . nothing indecent I just want to be close to you until we can find out what the hell is going on."

Marge said, "I will be glad to come home with you, I really don't want to be alone." Jim went, "My daughter was here for two days last week and cleaned the house and she washed up the bedding in the spare bedroom, ah, I don't want to let you out of my sight, I know this will sound crazy but I, oh well, Darn it I want you with me and not alone tonight, Okay?" Marge said, "Jim, I have not had sex with anyone since Al died, so for the time being this has to be a platonic relationship." Jim made a sound in his throat, "God woman, I'm not sure if I could have sex with any woman, I just kind of kept myself real busy since Mary died, sex has been the last thing on my mind, and you are safe with me. I have some steaks in the deep freeze, could you rustle us up some supper while I do chores?"

They stopped at Marge's so she could gather up a few clothes and things. When they got out to the ranch, she made a meal from what she could find in the kitchen. After supper they watched T.V. like two old married folks.

CHAPTER 16

SUNDAY NIGHT

BURT DROVE UP FOR Lorinda as promised, she had spent the afternoon painting, she finished one painting and already started another. She had agonized over what to wear until Molly said, "Wear the outfit you wore to lunch today you look so cute in that."

When they drove off Lorinda said, "The fresh air and quiet must have inspired me I painted up a storm and I think they're pretty good."

Burt and Lorinda talked non-stop all through dinner. They found a lot in common to talk about; their dreams and hope for their children and what they themselves wanted out of life.

Burt and Lorinda laughed all the way through the movie. Afterwards they drove to an all night truck stop for coffee. As they sat down, Lorinda looked up to see Julie Denning and a very nice looking young man walk in. Julie came right over, Lorinda said, "Sit with us."

Julie introduced Blake Denton. Everyone seemed comfortable except Blake, who kept looking at Burt with a puzzled look on his face. After a few minutes Burt said, "I'm going to find the little boys room." Blake jumped up, "Me too." In the restroom, Blake said, "What the hell's going on? I know who you are!" Burt said eyes flashing, "Forget you ever saw me!" Both men walked back to the table not speaking. After visiting mostly with Lorinda and Julie, Burt said to Lorinda, "It's getting late, I hate to, but we had better go." Julie hugged Lorinda and Blake shook both their hands still with same strange look on his face.

As they drove home Lorinda couldn't take her eyes off this man. He seemed to feel the same way about her, but Lorinda knew other men have liked her for awhile, then disappeared; so she didn't get to excited.

Arriving home she opened her door, he rushed around to help her out, managing to take her in his arms. A warm kiss later Lorinda in her blunt way said, "Goodbye, you are the most wonderful man . . . I think . . . hesitant, you're also handsome and fun. I don't want to get hurt again, but it sure would be easy to fall madly in love with you." No answer, he just sort of grabbed her as close as possible, his head in her hair. He kissed her again, walked back to his S.U.V. blew her a kiss and said, "You won't get hurt by me, then drove off smiling. Lorinda floated into her childhood home, she felt like a teenager again does he love me does he love me not. In just a few hours Lorinda's life would be far more complicated than a kiss from technically a stranger.

CHAPTER 17

SHERIFF BRIAN STAYED UP until Julie came singing in the house. It was obvious he was fuming, "Julie, this guy is one of those bleeding heart counselors, that think all prisoners are telling the truth; STAY AWAY FROM HIM; I'm the bad guy to him." "Dad I'm having fun who says this will lead to anything, but I do really like him." Brian said, "Mark my words, he's not for you, and stomped off to bed. She hugged herself in her bedroom thinking, I more than like him!!

CHAPTER 18

BLAKE DENTON CALLED WILL States from his motel room. "I know it's late, I had a wonderful and . . . . weird day. This Sheriff Dennings daughter is . . . . I don't know . . . my soul mate I guess. We spent the afternoon and evening together. I met the Sheriff, the Judge and the States Attorney over grilled salmon, they were so . . . nice, too nice; maybe it's me, but they seem to be a lot richer than other public officials I know. I think I know what DCF stands for—Denning, Calder, and Fresman. I'm confused, I sound jealous, but there is something, well, not right, they're just too damn smooth. I'm pretty accurate on what makes people tick. Also Julie confided in me—when I asked if criminals ever came after her or her mother; she said, "After many threats, her Dad built a safe place for them under the greenhouse. They have a key, but never go in because it has an alarm hooked to the Sheriff's office; get this, only Brian uses it." Plus there's more, I met someone last night with a friend of Julie's. I can't tell you who it was yet . . . . until I check something out. I think I know him and I can't figure out how he plays in all this!"

At midnight Blake's cell phone rang, he thought "Julie." Instead it was Burton Knight. Blake amazed, "How did you get my cell number?" Burt interrupted, "I'm sorry, I understood you are visiting Julie's aunt in the morning, is there some way you could manage to get Julie to bring you over to my ranch first?" Blake blew up, "What the hell's going on. I can't believe this weekend; you were so cold last night; like we never met before. I feel like my mind is whirling with information, I can't put it together and to add to all this . . . is meeting a girl I fell in love with at first sight. I think I'm losing my mind!!!" Burt said, "Whoa; it will take me awhile to lay all this out to you, I hate doing it on the phone and I'm giving you secret information. You absolutely have to keep my confidence. AGREED?"

Burt and Blake talked for an hour, at the end of their conversation, Burt was grim. Then Blake remembered, "Oh I forgot, I thought I recognized your Lorinda's name. I'm sure she is kind of a famous landscape artist in Sioux Falls. Her paintings are displayed in an old stable, they made into an art gallery,; her name is so unusual." Burt breathed a sigh of relief, "Oh, please tell Julie this; insist on going to Lorinda's folks place first, please, I'm sorry I can't tell you why."

CHAPTER 19

MONDAY MORNING

LAURA DENNING GOT UP early to fix a grumpy Brian Denning breakfast. He said, "I have to hurry or I'd get Julie up and lecture her about this Denton kid! You tell her—I mean it—that I don't like him!" Laura tired, "Well after listening to you last night ranting and raving about him; first to me, than Julie . . . I guess we both know how YOU FEEL!" She put on her jacket and gloves and went out to the greenhouse. She thought, Brian acts like he loves Julie and I, but only if we do what he wants. He's like a spoiled brat; wanting everything with no problems. He can't seem to get enough—new cars, this house, all his big boy toys; but happy he's not! Then she stopped herself—thinking about all his good qualities. He spared no expense for her or Julie anything they wanted . . . . if it could be bought.

Julie called out, "Mom, I'm up and ready to go." Laura hurried to the kitchen, "I'll fix you some breakfast. What's the big hurry?" Julie blushed, "I'm going to meet Blake in town and we're following each other back east; stopping at Aunt Vanna's for breakfast." Laura distressed, "Oh, Julie I hope your Dad is gone by then; He seems to . . . well . . . . he just don't like that boy!' Why don't you call Vanna and say you got up late?" "No," Julie firm, "Dad is more controlling every year— for crying out loud Mom-can't you see-he don't want—anyone—around us—even Aunt Lou or Uncle Dave. I used to love big family gatherings with my cousins. How long has it been?"

For a minute Laura could see some of Brian in Julie: the self control and the "I'm right" attitude. Julie softened, "Mom I love you and Dad, but I wish just once you would stand up to him. Tell him to stick it where the sun don't shine! All he seems to care about is how we look to outsiders—the perfect wife and daughter!""Well", Laura said, "He is the sheriff and he needs to look perfect in the voter's minds, that's why he is so careful." Julie, "I'm going to meet Blake anyway, that's it, and we are going to Aunt Vanna's, she will love him!" Laura privately thought, "Yeah, Julie, Vanna likes all—men.

A pickup drove up the driveway as Julie was leaving. She said, "Oh, Mr. Addington is here; Hi; only it was a different landscape man. Laura said, "Goodness I didn't know you were coming today, ah, I thought tomorrow! Julie, this is Pete Kall, he is replacing Addington—who's trying to retire." Pete shook Julie's hand and then hurried off to the garden shed. Laura puzzled, "I was sure it was tomorrow, he's going to help me wrap the birch trees, so the deer don't kill them." Julie looked at her mother as Laura took her scarf off and fluffed up her hair. Julie said, "You like him, Wow! It never hurts to take a look around you, huh?" Julie burst out with her sweet laugh "I can't believe it!" Laura embarrassed, "Stop that, he is a retired Air Force Sergeant, learning the landscape business, he lives in an apartment now, but is looking for a house in the Black Hills. Yes, I guess I really like him. He is so interested in my plants and flowers, she laughed then, "He walks ramrod straight like march 1-2-3-. I think he even presses his work pants. He looks like Gregory Peck, from my young movie days." She playfully swatted Julie's arm, "Darn it, he's my friend!" Julie threw her arms around Laura giving her a bear hug, teasing-rolling her eyes, "Have fun." Laura watched Julie drive off and then joined the sergeant. He said, "What a beautiful girl."

CHAPTER 20

Julie drove up to Blake's motel and waited while he checked out. She told him, "We will be taking a back road to my Aunt's it's some unusual country, very isolated, we'll talk on our cell phones; keep my car in sight." Blake said, "Is it possible to stop and see Lorinda Kemp first, I think she is an artist from Sioux Falls and I would like to visit with her for a few minutes. Would that be alright?" "Sure, Julie said, "That will be fun I'll call Molly and see if their home. I'm sure they are though."

After they had went a ways, Julie turned off on a side road; suddenly Highway Patrol cars, Sheriff cars and fire trucks flew by them. Julie called Blake, "I can't believe this; there is never traffic on this road, something must have happened!"

A few more miles down the road, at the top of a hill sat a patrol car. When they drove up, he came to Julie's car and said, "You'll have to turn back, there's been an accident, go back two miles then two miles north, there's another road going east.

Julie could see smoldering smoke-prairie fire-she thought—then she seen a van blown apart . . . on a door laying off to the side she could see Sheriff . . . right below her. She jumped out of the car, the patrolman tried to stop her, but she shoved him back. She started screaming, "That's my Dad's van—That's my Dad's van—he was transporting a prisoner down this road, this morning!" She ran crying and screaming down the hill. Blake didn't know what to do, he sprinted around the cop and tore down the hill after her. There were two black body bags on the ground and debris everywhere. Two firemen grabbed Julie as she struggled, "My Dad is Brian Denning, this is his sheriff's van. He was coming this way to my Aunt Vanna's. LET ME LOOSE_-LET GO OF ME!" Blake panting stood to the side. A deputy came up to him, "It is her Dad and deputy, the prisoner is missing, we are trying to find him. Can you get her out of here?" Blake asked, "Does she know you, can you help me tell her?"

"Yes." the deputy said. By then Julie was on her knees by a body bag, hysterical. Blake and the deputy lifted her to her feet. Vanna and Dale Schultz came running to hold Julie. Vanna kept moaning over and over, "I can't believe it, Drake saw the smoke and found all this—they called us." Doug and Nina are with your mother, Judge Calder's on his way to get you."

The deputy came up and asked if maybe they could go to Vanna's. He asked Blake to drive Julie's car to her Aunt's; then he would bring him back for his car. Blake couldn't believe his eyes as he followed the deputy to Vanna's. Everything looked barren until they got to the ranch. What a magnificent place! Blake got in with the deputy, "My God, what a mess, can you tell me what happened?" The deputy grim, "There was some kind of small propane tank, like for a grill, in fact two or three of them, blew up by the van (I don't know) and we can't find this convict kind of a crazy kid." He might be laying dead somewhere; maybe he did this . . . I just don't know . . . Old man Denning had a deer rifle in his fried hand." The deputy choked up, "What a f—, excuse me—to see him like that! Sorry; it was bad and Damon, the deputy with him; like (Oh, God) there was nothing left of him!" They're describing this prisoner as armed and dangerous; I just don't know as he wiped his eyes."

Blake got in his car and immediately grabbed his cell phone to call Burt Knight. No answer, Surely Burt had nothing to do with blowing up a Sheriff and his deputy, what had he meant, when he said something was going down on one of these ranches and he wanted me to keep Julie away, My God Blake thought, "What do I do now." He decided to drive back to Julie's Aunts place and see if he could help Julie.

CHAPTER 21

JIM BALL WOKE UP to someone taking a shower and for a minute couldn't figure out, who, then he remembered—Marge—she was up and dressed by the time he got out of his own shower. He said, "In a hurry are we." Marge threw her arms around him and kissed him, I slept like a log, thank you I slept so good last, I don't know I felt safe I guess, these last two weeks has drained me dry. I'm sorry we had to meet under such strange circumstances." Jim held her so tight she couldn't catch her breath for a few minutes. When he let go of her he said, "I so want to help you, ah, I know what an ornery old cuss your dad is and I can tell this is like a nightmare to you, only you wake up to find out it's real." Marge said, "Dad's not only ornery he is so tight with money, it's awful, but he did go with me to see Joel in prison and he cried for the first hundred miles home, I was so shocked, I still don't know if it was because Joel was in prison or if he was worried what people would say. He made, Barry, my brother pay an arm and a leg for that farm, poor Barry, I don't care as much as Barry does-what the old fart thinks—he has never helped me out with a nickel through all my trouble and I don't want his damn money anyway, but guess what he can't take it with him, so we probably will be wealthy kids someday. Enough about him, my first concern is Joel.

Jim said, "I thought we could stop in Middleborg and talk to Sheriff Denning, let's take a thermos of coffee and stop at the bakery. Then maybe we can drive straight through to this AL's Diner. Does that sound like a plan to you?"

They visited all through the drive, stopping in front of the Haines County Sheriff's office. He said, "I'll go in unless you want to?" "She said horrified, "No, I came here many times I don't like him, he acts so nice, but I don't think he is, he was no help at all!"

The dispatch lady said, "The sheriff just left with a prisoner for Sioux Falls, but one of the deputies can help you." The deputy said, "We all tried to tell Joel his story didn't make sense, but he insisted. Judge Calder went easy on him. We're sure sorry to hear he jumped parole and seems to be missing."

Jim said to Marge in the pickup, "Your right not much help and that deputy acted like a smart ass!" Jim went on, even though he didn't say it, he looked smug or something. He shrugged, "Kind of strange, shifty eyes like some crook, I have met a few in my time. I don't know how to describe the feeling I got from him." Marge said, "Now you know what I mean."

CHAPTER 22

EARLY MONDAY MORNING

WHEN JIM AND MARGE drove away from the Haines County Sheriff's office: Deputy Flann was watching-standing back from the window-so they couldn't see him. He went back to the Sheriffs empty office and used his cell phone to call someone. "Yeah, I thought you had better know; that Joel Moss's mother was here with Sheriff Jim Ball from Willis—she didn't come in—he did—asking a lot of questions. I've heard he's like a bull dog when it comes to solving a case. Tougher than Hell. He's going out toward old Turtle Mountain, he got some kind of tip about Joel's car and get this—when he got in his pickup—he reached over and kissed old lady Moss! Well I thought you should know; I'm telling you I don't like this one bit, especially if Ball is looking into things."

CHAPTER 23

MONDAY MORNING EARLY

LORINDA AND MOLLY BOTH got up about the same time, Molly said, "You could have slept in, the chores can wait awhile." Lorinda yawning, "I couldn't sleep. Mom I had such a good time last night. The only thing is I like this Burt Knight way too much and damn, damn, I wish I didn't, too many times I've been disappointed about the men in my life!" Molly said, "He's a good man. Even your Dad thinks the world of him." "Yeah, I know Mom, but it happened again, that kind of secret side of him, that shows on his face. You've seen it. Molly slowly nodded. Well, last night we stopped at the truck stop cafe in Rapid City after the movie. I couldn't believe my eyes when I looked up and saw Julie Denning come in with some handsome young man. She was just blooming as she introduced him, Blake somebody; he is a counselor at the Sioux Falls State Prison and—get this—I could have sworn he knew Burt before. This kid explained he was here to visit the mother of a prisoner who was out on parole and now was missing. He had visited Sheriff Brian at his house, I guess Brian invited him for Sunday dinner. He told Julie he had never seen Mount Rushmore so Julie offered to take him there. They had went to the same movie as us. I thought to myself, they couldn't seem to take their hands off each other; love at first sight or something. Anyway, when he wasn't looking in Julie's eyes, he was staring at Burt with a funny look on his face. It made me uncomfortable; Burt acted like he didn't notice. I guess I wondered why Burt would know a prison counselor; I'll admit a few things ran through my mind. Remember when I was young this boy asked me out, drove clear out here to the ranch and picked me up, even you thought he was nice, but

Tom found out he had a criminal record from the time he was thirteen years old, boy I got rid of him fast." Molly laughed "You have always been sensitive, you pick up on things about people before other's would even notice it. That's probably why you're a good supervisor at work." Molly got up, "I think I'll make some baking powder biscuits and we'll have biscuits and gravy for breakfast and maybe a pan of monkey bread, you never know . . . . maybe your honey will stop over sometime today, if he's not a hardened criminal, I think your imagination might be running away with you, ha!" Lorinda said, "Yeah I know, I'm kind of leery about people until I know everything about them. He did tell me he was going to invite me over to his place, but I was not to look at the house. He said he was still fixing up the outside buildings and fences and stuff. I felt dumb when he told me after hearing Vanna talk about my house, that he wondered if he should let me see how he lives. I guess he has two hired men and they all live in the house, so it's kind of a bachelor pad, whatever that means. I told him my house is nice, but nothing like Vanna's and I would love to see his place. On the other hand I might never see him again, who knows?" Molly said, "I'll come with you to milk this morning, it is just beautiful out, the sun is already up and it feels warm already, I'll leave the biscuits ready to bake the monkey bread is quick to make so we'll bake it while we eat breakfast." Oh," Lorinda said, "I forgot to tell you about this goofy movie we saw last night it was hilarious, we both laughed and laughed." Molly stopped mixing dough for a minute and puzzled," Did you hear the porch door just now?" Lorinda went to look and said, "I think it was the cat, she wants some fresh milk; only look, her hair is all bristled up like she's mad I'm so late." Molly put the cat out and said, "How did you get in, Mrs. Muff, I swear she can open that door now, she gets into everything."

It was another gorgeous fall morning-cool—they both put on jackets, "Mom I love this peaceful quiet place, even though it's dry and barren here." They both stopped in their tracks, they could see smoke; lots of smoke, to the south. Molly upset, "I wish the neighbors would not burn, when it's so dry. Vanna always has fire over there, her stupid chiminea's. Oh, that might be the Drake's maybe their burning junk, I wish they wouldn't this time of year. We'll keep an eye on it, maybe we had better go see what's burning." Lorinda said, "Oh look it's dying down now, well kind of. Can we wait until I do chores?" Molly looking toward the smoke, "I think your right it is dying down, good." Katie cow came up to the barn door, as Lorinda opened it she looked out o see Daisy horse, standing by the other barn door, blood running down her side. Lorinda yelled, "Mom come quick Daisy's hurt!" The old horse stood quiet while Lorinda ran her hands all over her. Where's she bleeding from, I can't find a thing, not even a scratch!" Molly said, "Well my goodness, look at those goofy calves, usually you can't beat them off with a stick, now they all ran to the other side of the barn. I'll clean Daisy up while you milk." Lorinda put Katie cow in the stanchion and sat down to milk. Molly came in and pulled up a grain pail to sit on. She said "You never know in this country what goes on, just like Daisy, I can't even guess what happened to her and why does someone have to burn in this dry weather?"

Lorinda still milking started talking about the awful prairie fires when she was a kid. "One thing, that was good about it, she said, "was we got out of school to help wet down gunny sacks, so the adults could beat out the flames that got past where all the neighbor men had plowed in front of the fire. I guess I could live without all that." She looked up to see Molly staring at something, trying to get off her pail, an alarmed scowling look on her face. "WHO ARE YOU, WHAT IN THE WORLD?" Lorinda jumped up standing behind her was a young man, in her Dad's old coat; Holding a 22 long rifle; blood was dripping from one sleeve, it looked like his face was sunburned; no; blistered-eyebrows gone, grotesque, like a Halloween mask. Shaking all over he said, "I want the keys to that car out there or I'll shoot you!" He staggered, then leaned up against the wall, "I MEAN IT, YOU MUST HAVE THE KEYS ON YOU, I CAN'T FIND THEM IN THE HOUSE!" Molly and Lorinda looked at each other with horror. Lorinda said, "WHAT IN GOD'S NAME HAPPENED TO YOU AND WHO ARE YOU?" "What the Hell is going on?" Molly yelled, "YOUNG MAN YOU ARE OBVIOUSLY IN A LOT OF PAIN! PLEASE, FOR GOD'S SAKE, SIT DOWN. We will help you, just sit down." He growled like an animal, "Get me those keys!" He was trying to stand in front of them, weaving all over like a drunk. Suddenly, behind this creature stood Burton Knight, his fingers to his lips with a gun in his hand. Lorinda calmly looked at the young man and said, "Young man that's my old rabbit shooting rifle your holding. It's missing a firing pin . . . . so guess what: you couldn't possibly shoot anyone with it. NOW SIT DOWN RIGHT NOW!"

Burt, Molly and Lorinda watched as the boy went sliding down the wall. He began weeping, sorrow seeping out of every pore in his body; sobbing almost incoherent," I made crystal meth, yes, but I didn't do anything else and no one, but no one is going to believe me. This morning at 6:00 I was picked up by Sheriff Denning at the Haines County Jail-another prisoner got in with us; (Damon). We were both handcuffed in the back seat of the Sheriff's van—a cage between us and the front seat. We stopped in an alley, behind a store, where the sheriff loaded some garbage bags and three small propane tanks, like for a grill, in the back of the van. When he got back in he said, "Boys we're going to drop some groceries at my sister's and have coffee with some homemade rolls, it will be a nice break for all of us." "I asked Damon what he did and he said, "I robbed a bank; shut up." I said "Do you smell something funny, a weird smell, like some kind of gas, after I thought, it smelled like anhydrous ammonia, what the hell the sheriff was doing with anhydrous, I couldn't figure out and in little propane bottles plus that was no grocery store he stopped at, I kept this thought to myself, Damon looked at me, "Didn't I tell you to shut up?" I tried not to show it, but I recognized his eyes, when he looked direct at me, he's the one with the mask that drove me and other pharmacy students, to a secret meth Lab! I got a funny creepy feeling trying to figure all this out. You see, I had confessed to Sheriff Denning and the States Attorney, also a Judge. I asked them to help me find this lab and put a stop to it. I told them I must have been insane to have got involved, but it was just so . . . . much money. I knew I would never get a pharmaceutical license from college if I got caught so I tried to solve things by reporting it; hoping to cut a deal. Instead I got in more trouble. The three of them said I would have to serve time and they assured me this meth lab would be found and if I would plead guilty and serve time, they would get it erased from my record. My folks stepped in and hired an attorney, too late I guess, because he finally said, "Go along with this until I can figure out this mess." Another attorney had told him about a Joel Moss who ended up in prison for the same deal I did; only thing this Joel got out, but no one can find him, he like just disappeared. Any way the sheriff took some back road, in a pretty desolate area, like no houses, just up and down hills. After an hour or more, He said, "I got to take a leak, how about you boys?' He pulled over to the side of the road, took off my handcuffs; then Damon's. I said, "Sir, there's a smell coming from the back, like gas or something. "He said, "It's an old van probably just exhaust from an old pipe, maybe a small hole in it. I'll check when we stop at my sister's place." Suddenly he says, "Hey, I see an antelope up on the hill, so he lifts a deer rifle off the rack in the van window, looking through the scope. I started to walk toward the ditch to pee, when I felt like they were watching me. Then I just knew that smell was anhydrous, and it is one of the main ingredients in crystal meth. The sheriff said, "Now, Todd you stay close to me, don't try to run away. I want to get a closer look at this antelope, kind of walk behind me while I sneak up this hill." Damon was watching us with hard cold eyes, I thought it's barely daylight; he didn't see any antelope . . . . they're going to shoot me and say I tried to run. I stood by the van, terrified, then he pointed the rifle straight at me—I jumped in the ditch just as he pulled the trigger. I will swear on a stack of Bibles, when he shot, the van blew in a million pieces. I ended up in a barbed wire ence. "The boy stopped, his whole body shivering. Molly and Lorinda rushed to him taking off their jackets, as Burt did wrapping the boy up. His head shaking, making his words sound like stutters said, "I know you don't believe me, no one will." Burt said, "Young man—I'm not just a rancher I am a DEA agent (Drug Enforcement Agency) listen to me; see this thing in my hand it's a sophisticated camera phone, taking down everything you say. There's a Medivac helicopter on its way for you." The boy screamed trying to stand up, "No, they will kill me!" Burt said, "Listen please there are two FBI agents right outside this barn (Come in guys) one will be going with you. Your attorney, Will States and your parents have already been notified. They will be waiting at the hospital."

Both Molly and Lorinda looked at Burt and the two men like they were from outer space. "What made you come here—Burt?" Burt said, "I seen the smoke this morning I went to investigate and they said a prisoner escaped, I won't say what else—I thought the two of you are alone and I saw blood and skin on the fence going north, you were this way." Kindly he turned to the young man, whose eyes were full of . . . hope, tears rolling down his poor burned face. Burt said to the boy, "And how did you get here so fast-Todd Ames?" The boy whispered, "You know me?" The boy went on; it was like slow motion, fire everywhere, I seen their bodies fly in the air . . . on fire. I was burnt and bleeding, the barbed wire stuck in my back. Things kept exploding by the van, that's when I tore loose from the fence and started running up the hill, I was in such terrible pain, my lungs were on fire, at least that's how they felt, over the hill I saw some horses, they were standing by a water tank; I climbed in; at first it felt good, then I felt frozen. A Palomino horse (I think) walked up to me with a halter on, she nudged me with her nose. I knew I had to get help or hide or something. I grabbed the horse's mane and halfway climbed on; she carefully carried me to this barn "Like an Angel from Heaven" embarrassed he said, "You see I prayed to God over and over; save me; he did!"

Burt with an agonized look on his face said, "Molly and Lorinda, I'm so sorry, please, please, forgive me. I have very little time to explain. Today was "D" day-there are about a hundred agents in this area right now. We finally have proof enough to send a lot of people to jail. Everything finally came together on Sunday while we were in church. My men finally found an underground meth lab after six months of searching. Last year we got a clue as to how professional perfect meth was showing up all over the USA and foreign countries. A western store in South America was selling meth shipped from South Dakota. It was found in boxes and bags of saddles, the meth enclosed in bubble wrap. Molly and Lorinda gasped. "Yes", Burt said "you guessed, but we could only find how it was shipped. We have searched this whole area for a lab. Our first break came two weeks ago when our satellite picture picked up an unbelievable scene; it still took until Sunday, for my people to find the lab. It is so clever and genius, how it was built. The one thing we didn't expect was for Brian Denning to blow himself up; he was to be arrested this morning, now everything is messed up. I am retiring after this mess, I came to search this country for a methamphetamine lab and ended up finding the Olson place for sale I loved it on sight and decided to settle here permanently. I wish I could tell you more, it's a secret operation.

CHAPTER 24

LAURA AND PETE KALL spent about an hour unrolling and cutting the wrap for the trees. Laura felt so content, what a beautiful day and how nice it was to work with this easy going man. He seemed to enjoy being outside. Suddenly Laura's heart started racing, she felt like a dark cloud had descended right over her head. She shivered, "Pete concerned, "Are you all right?" She said, "I'm going in to make some lunch." As she took off her gloves, sweat broke out all over her body, she thought I'm AFRAID—this is fear in my body. What in the world! . . . Julie . . . she thought, worried she rushed to the phone—only to see what looked like Doug and Nina Fresman drive in; Megan with them. Laura felt ice cold as she opened the door. She knew something was terribly wrong.

Meanwhile, Pete Kall outside wondered what was going on. He distinctly heard someone crying, not sure what to do he kept wrapping trees. A tall brassy, looking blonde woman came outside and lit a cigarette. Walking toward him, like a model on a runway, very pretty, she said, "Can I ask who you are? A friend of Laura's (looking at him with heavily lined eyes) a lover or what?" she snickered!" He stood up ramrod straight, "I'm the new landscape man and I don't appreciate the insolence!" He turned his back to her. She took a puff, "You don't look like a gardener to me, but what do I know? Look, I'm not trying to be rude or anything, but could you kind of disappear? Mrs. Denning's husband was killed in an accident this morning, it's pretty sad." Pete whirled, "What did you say? An accident where? I mean it's none of my business!" He flushed, Megan said, "His van blew up is all we know so far, except he is dead." Pete, "I'll just put this roll away, will you please tell Mrs. Denning how sorry I am?" Megan was standing by a big fancy car as Pete drove off. He drove up the driveway out of sight, then he pushed the talk button on his ear phone, "Did you hear all that?" Someone answered, "Man what else can go wrong I thought we had this all planned and timed perfect!" Pete musing, "You know what this might work out better. I'll come up there with you."

CHAPTER 25

BLAKE DENTON DROVE BACK to Vanna's wondering what to do. When he got back to the ranch, Julie came out still sobbing. Blake felt so helpless. He kept quiet when she said, "He left this morning mad at me!" Reluctantly Blake asked "Julie was your Dad mad at you about me . . . . Maybe he didn't like me?" This brought on fresh sobs. In the house Vanna sat by the kitchen table looking about a hundred years old. She was staring straight ahead. They introduced him to Mary Pringle, who looked helpless too. He could see four men outside smoking, shaking their heads. He said, "Julie I feel like an outsider infringing on your families private grief. Why don't I go back to town? I'll stay another night and call you tomorrow?" Julie threw her arms around him, "I feel like I've known you all my life, I'll call you as soon as we get all this sorted out. Please Blake stay in town at least one more night." Blake recognized the tall distinguished white haired man, who rushed up to Julie hugging her, tears running down his face. Blake said, "I can't tell you how sorry I am for all of you, nice to see you again, Judge." Suddenly Vanna jumped up swinging her hands to sweep all the dishes off the table, glass shattering everywhere. They all stood mute and shocked. Blake more uncomfortable than ever. Judge Calder said, "Brace up Vanna we can't do anything about it. God how I wish we could change this day. Julie your mother wants you to call, use my cell phone, Mary can you clean this up and get us some coffee; I know I sure need some!" Vanna fell in the Judge's arms through tears she howled, "Without Brian there's nothing to live for!" Judge Calder rocked her back and forth whispering in her ear until the crazed look on her face eased up. Julie on the phone was trying to talk to Laura, neither were coherent. Mary Pringle straightened things up and with a strange fearful look on her face, "Vanna, I think we will go home, ah, there's not much we can do here, I need to at least get my hair combed!" Pringle's and Blake left.

Blake got in his car thinking, "My God what a day!" Blake's cell phone rang as soon as he got in his car. It was Will States, "Where have you been? Everything is crazy here you won't believe this; real off the wall shit going on!" Blake kept saying, "Holy Cow I can't believe all this, Will, this is nuts. Blake felt completely drained as he sat listening to Will States story. When he finally got a word or two in besides saying, Holy Cow about ten times, "I'm going to hang up and see if I can get a hold of Burton Knight. I've tried all morning. I'll call you back." Burt picked up on the first ring, "Blake, I saw your number on my caller. I.D. but couldn't answer right then, how much do you know about all this and where is Julie Denning? I would like you to drive over to the O'Malley's and hurry up please I don't want Lorinda or her mother here alone and I have got to go, I'll tell you what I know as you drive and then I'll put you on speaker, so the rest of the team can hear your input." Blake close to tears trying not to be emotional, "Started telling his story, talking and driving, as he topped a hill he started yelling, "Oh-My-God-Burt, Oh-My-God, I just found Joel's Turtle Mountain, still yelling, I can see it plain as day!!" In a sad tired voice Burt said, "You and your Joel helped us solve a mystery, we have spent two months trying to locate. Burt went on, "Denton your call to Bob Allard, Saturday night, finally helped us locate the Lab, if and we really can't say if, in this business, but if we had known the Lab was located by Turtle Mountain before, we would have had a two month jump on this investigation. I nearly had a heart attack when we met you with Denning's daughter, of all people, at that truck stop Sunday night, then you started telling what a wonderful lunch you had at Sheriff Denning's house, I just about fell off my chair. You might say I was worried. Look I have to go, come here as soon as you can, I have two ladies standing in their barn, who are looking at me like I'm the Devil or a monster, they are having trouble believing Denning was an asshole."

CHAPTER 26

SHERIFF JIM BALL AND Marge Moss were on the road to Placerville, Marge started telling him all she had went through trying to find help for Joel. She said, "I didn't even get him an attorney; Joel pled guilty because the States Attorney told him it would be the best way to go and then they would get it off his record, after a few months of parole. While Joel was in prison though he found other young men that had been supposedly helped by this so called States Attorney and they insisted he was a crook himself." Jim Ball was weighing all this information in his head plus some things he had heard in the past about Haines County Law, being a good-old-boy society.

AL's Place turned out to be about two hours away. When they got there they ordered breakfast and Jim identified himself to the waitress, she went and got Al. While they ate Al sat in a booth with them describing Joel's car in detail sheepishly he said, "I had one just like it when I was a kid. They asked him his impressions of the neighboring ranches. He said, "Their few and far between. All the folks are hard working, from sun up to sun down taking care of cattle and some crops mostly hay. They're all good people."

Going outside with them he pointed, "When you get to the top of hill from my place; you can see old Turtle Mountain. You will come to a cross road, turn right, that will take you to Dale and Vanna Schultz's place or Lester Pringle's. If you go left, it's O'Malleys. I did see a line of smoke north of here; I'm going to go up there myself to see what that's about after I get caught up here." Jim and Marge thanked him several times for calling in news of Joel.

Jim and Marge drove north from AL's Diner. At the top of the hill they could see a lot of smoke to their left. They both commented on how barren the land seemed, up and down hills, then ahead it looked like flat land. When Marge looked to the left, she nearly jumped off the pickup seat, grabbing Jim's arm she pointed, "Turtle Mountain, just like Joel said. Can you see it off to the east?" Jim couldn't believe it, then ahead a highway patrol car was blocking the road west. The patrolman came up to Jim's window, "Accident to the west, you can go north a couple of miles, then turn east again." Then he took off his sun glasses and looked closer at Jim, he said, "Are you Sheriff Jim Ball?" "Yes, what kind of accident, do you need some help?" The patrolman tipped his hat to Marge. "Ah, Jim could I talk to you for a few minutes?" Jim stepped out, the patrolman moving dirt back and forth with his boots, "Do you have your radio with you." "Sure!" "Well we have been ordered to keep radio silence, some federal guys were on top of this the minute we got here. I can't even go down to the accident site, boy their like blood hounds all over the place. All I can find out is they think it was Sheriff Denning from Haines County and his deputy blown up in a van, they had a prisoner, but they can't find him. I don't know what the hell to think. There's some kind of white powder blown all over. I heard one of the Feds say, chlorphmiramin and dextromethorphan."

Jim's head came up in surprise, "What's that stuff for, incredulous, it dawned on him, Do you mean meth?" "Yeah, I guess I can't figure it out, what in the world Denning had this junk in the van for, well, I can't for the life of me figure it out." Jim taking his hat off and running a hand over his brow, an angry look on his face, "Look I have Marge Moss with me, her son was accused of making and selling crystal meth and he told her by a Turtle Mountain or hill or some damn thing, well over there sure as hell looks like turtle mountain to me. Marge, called me and said the kid was missing almost as soon as he got out of jail, and he insisted some big shots had to be involved in this secret underground lab, to tell you the truth I kind of doubted the kid myself, but now I'm beginning to wonder!" The patrol scratched his head, "An underground meth lab, where; by this turtle mountain?" "Yes," Jim said, "I don't know anything for sure, but my guess we're involved in something big here." They both heard the whap, whap of a helicopter over head, looking like it was going to land to the east. The patrolman ran to his car he said, "Dispatch, do you know anything about a helicopter?" "Hell No, we are out of the loop I guess because we can't find out what going on there." Then Jim could see Medivac on the side of the helicopter. He said, "I'll go see and call you. What's your cell number there must still be radio silence. Jim jumped in the pickup following the helicopter with his eyes, he turned east; Marge sat looking worried at the grim look on Jim's face, he looked furious, "Marge, I don't know what kind of mess we are driving into, I just wish I had checked Joel's story out before, I think that boy uncovered a nest of human rattlesnakes, I pray to God he lived through it." Arriving at a mailbox that said O'Malley, two black vested men stood with guns. They had a car stopped. One man walked back to Jim and said, "Move along folks!" Then the man from the car got out and ran back to them. Shock registered, Jim looked at Marge, "My God it's that Denton from Sioux Falls, dirty smudged up looking, what happened to you, I mean how the,—well—how could you be here." Blake said to the two men, "This is a Sheriff, I will vouch for them, call Burton Knight, he will let us in." After a few minutes, they told them to go ahead. Blake waved, "Follow me I'll fill you in when we get there." Up the long driveway sat the helicopter, an older woman and a younger woman both dressed in what looked like chore clothes, the younger woman kept trying to straighten her hair with her hands, they were walking on either side of stretcher holding someone's hand it appeared. Two white uniformed were carrying the stretcher with what looked like a pile of rags on it. The women moved as the E.M.T.'S put the stretcher on the helicopter, they stood with their arms around each other. The helicopter took off; three black SUV's were turning ready to leave, a tall black haired man hurried over to Blake. Blake explained who Jim and Marge were. "Oh, God Burt said. Blake grabbed Burt's arm, shaking all over—desperate-, "Burt please, please tell me, are Julie and Laura Denning involved in any of this?" Burt said, "We don't think so, they're going to be questioned and of course all their assets frozen; but, no we don't think they knew a thing about it." Blake nearly burst into tears. Burt put his arm around him, "Love her, huh?" Well I have to get moving, there's a lot of people to catch up to yet." Burt called to Jim Ball and asked if he had his gun with him." Jim shook his head yes, ah can you tell us what's going on here?" Burt said, Blake will fill you in on what he knows and I would like both you and Blake to stay here with the women that live here I hope they're not in any danger, but I'm not sure, they're friends with all the people involved and I don't want someone to try to get them to help escape or as hostages." Blake asked then Burton is Bob Allard here?" "Yes, he is in Middleborg arresting some people as we speak and he does want to visit with you later." Blake said, "Ah, are you in charge, Burt, of the whole operation?""No, just this end of it, Sam Davis from Washington D.C. is in charge of the whole mess, Thank God, he's been flying around in an air force helicopter for three days lining up locations etc."

Burt was just ready to climb in a SUV when suddenly he rushed up to Lorinda clasping her face in his hands he said, "Don't forget me, okay, I'm going to be one busy man for a while, believe me, I can't forget you. Molly could you do me a favor and call Frank and ask him if he could run my ranch for maybe two months, my calves are not worked yet and they need to be weaned, my hired men are D.E.A. agents too, so they will be gone, Do you think Frank could find some help, money is no issue, whatever he thinks, I will pay." Molly still in shock, "You bet Burt, I'll call Frank today, I know he will be glad to help, I wish I knew what all is going to happen, but I gather you're not going to tell us." "No, Burt said, "I really don't want you to know, Blake can I speak to you in private a few minutes, I need you to tell Mrs. Moss her son is presumed dead, we have not recovered his body yet, but we believe we know where it's at, this is more in your field, I do not want to tell that poor woman, ease into all right?" Jim and Marge got out stand by Blake as Burt jumped in a SUV wheels spinning, he was gone.

The five of them left stood looking at each other after Burt left. Looking closer at Blake she said, "Are you Julie's friend, Mom, I was telling you about him, I couldn't for the life of me figure out why Burt had such a strange reaction when we met you the other night and I could tell you kept looking at him so puzzled, well anyway I guess I kept wondering why Burt would know a prison counselor from Sioux Falls, boy, was I wrong I thought maybe Burt was a criminal or something." Molly shook Blake's hand, who said, "Oh, I'm sorry this is Sheriff Jim Ball and Marge Moss from Willis, South Dakota, and I still have not found out what they're doing here, but I'm awful glad to see them." Lorinda surprised, "Moss, are you this Joel's mother?" Marge said, "Yes I am and how do you know that? Was that a body they were putting on that helicopter? WAS IT MY JOEL, PLEASE SOMEONE TELL ME WHAT'S GOING ON HERE, I'M ABOUT CRAZY STANDING HERE NOT KNOWING!" "Oh No," both Molly and Lorinda—No,—that was a boy named Todd Ames and he's going to be just fine." Marge looking bewildered at Jim, "Todd Ames, but that's the boy that lawyer has been calling me about." Molly sensing the hysteria in Marge's voice was not good suggested they all go in the house, she said, "I made fresh biscuits to put in the oven for what seems like a lifetime ago, let's go have some coffee while those biscuits bake and see if we can sort all this out." Marge whirled to Blake, "Joel's dead isn't he? Say it-damn it—I want to know!" Blake choked, "Yes." Marge laid her head on her arms bent over like she was having trouble breathing. Molly, Lorinda and Jim ran to her. Marge stood up straight, "I think I need that coffee now!" Settled around Molly's kitchen table Marge said to Blake, "Talk!" Sweat running down his face, "Their going to recover his body today if it's for sure him, before I go on I want you to know—Joel did not die in vain—because of him, the federal people finally found the crystal meth lab that was distributing meth almost all over the world.

Everyone listening gasped, "Where?" "I can't tell you because they didn't tell me where. What I can tell you is an enhanced satellite picture showed Joel's car (the unusual racing stripe) and two people, one of those two people shot him!" Lorinda looking at Molly questioning, "The Pringles, Oh, my God, Oh my God!" Blake said, "They won't tell me yet who shot him. Marge sat with her head on the table. Lorinda said to Blake, "So you did know Burton Sunday night?" "Yes, but he couldn't believe I was with Denning's daughter and he didn't want me to know anything. He thought I would tell Julie that Denning was going to be arrested this morning at his sister's place, I still don't know how he knew Denning would be there." Lorinda and Molly both said in unison, "We know how he knew we were all there for a Saturday night supper and Brian said he was he was coming over Monday morning, Burt heard it." Blake went on, "I wondered, Burt finally called me last night and asked me to keep Julie away from there well I guess you all know how that turned out."

Lorinda held up her hand, "Mom and I had a terrible experience this morning, I think it's time we told you what went on here first. After she finished telling about Todd Ames there was shocked silence. Jim ran his hands through his hair and Marge tears running down her face, "Did Denning shoot my boy—Blake? And how is it you are here?" Another long sad but scary story followed from Blake.

Molly and Lorinda both said, "Oh, we never thought about Vanna, how awful this must be for her, we should go over there soon, she just worships Brian, oh how awful and poor Laura." Jim uncomfortable said,

"Ah this Knight agent told me in no uncertain terms, we were all to stay right here." "Good grief" Lorinda said, "I haven't even finished chores yet!" Jim, "I'll tell you what we'll all help do chores when he gives the go ahead, okay." Blake talked then, "He told me it all has something to do with this Turtle Mountain and that the two of you might not be safe. Lorinda and Molly looked at each other "Turtle Mountain—but that's by—, well that can't be!" Molly said, "I always said those Damn Pringle boys were no good, they look just too slick." Mute for a few minutes the five of them were until Marge started telling her story. By now they were at least trying to eat the biscuits and gravy, Molly insisted food

CHAPTER 27

WHEN A BLACK CAR drove up to their very nice rock and log cabin, Dan went to the door. A man stood holding a badge, "Dan Danford?" "Yes." "You and your wife are under investigation for obstructing justice." Dan laughed, slapped his knee, "Holy Shit, Ma, come out here, some guy says he's going to take us to jail, he kept laughing. She came to the door, blinking in the sunshine, she asked, "Who are you, is this a joke?" The man said, "No, ma'am, I'm a DEA agent.' She blinked, "What's that?" He said "Drug Enforcement, we believe you have information concerning a methamphetamine lab run by students, who stay here during Spring break." The Danfords' looked at each other thinking (Joel again) they asked if they could call their attorney, we don't understand all this police talk." The man said, "That's fine I'll wait." Dan said, "Have a chair and a cup of coffee, we know about this crazy kid that keeps trying to find a scapegoat for his misdeeds." The man in black said, "I'll stand here and wait, thank you just the same." They called their attorney at home, shocked he said, "check their I.D.' "Well." Dan said, "We did and there's another one standing by the car with ATF or something on his jacket. The attorney asked to talk to the agent who gave him few details. He then told the Danford's, "Go with them, I'll meet you there, we'll clear this up right away."

After they dropped the Danford's off the ATF said, "They seem like a nice old couple." "You think how about their million dollar condo in Arizona, or all the other property they own only under a different name. Oh, their nice all right until they find out we know all about them; then we'll see!"

CHAPTER 28

MONDAY MORNING AT NIDDLEBORG college dormitory, Ted Heim and Sid Hess were getting ready for class. Ted was on the floor lifting weights before he showered. Sid had an early class—irritated—"Ted why do you have to do that now? I have to step over you or better yet on, YOU!" There was a knock at the door, Sid hurried by Ted, who was now standing up, for the bathroom. Ted took his time answering the door after a drink of water, he finally opened the door. A man in a dark suit said. "Ted Heim." "Yes." You're wanted for questioning in an investigation involving a meth lab." Ted smirked, "Oh, yeah, right." The man took a badge from his pocket, FBI, "Please come with me." Ted shocked, "What the hell am I under arrest or what?" "Just questioning downtown with some other folks." The man replied. Sid Hess coming out of the bathroom, heard the last few words, he threw down his towel and vaulted toward the man, trying to shove his way out the door. Another man standing in the hallway grabbed Sid's arms behind him and handcuffed him. "Sir, we have a warrant to search this room and to detain you downtown for questioning." Sid started to cry. Ted said, "Shut up, Sid they have the wrong guys, my folk will sue them for false arrest, search this room, we don't care!" The man in the suit, "Oh, Sonny boy we have more than a search warrant for this room, we can search your parents property too, guess what you all have a little too much money in the bank considering, none of you have jobs, you or your parents, believe me we have a mother lode of evidence against you. You can walk with me to the car— or —in handcuffs, I don't care either way, but you are coming with us!" Ted quietly walked with the agent, while Sid struggled with the other agent. Ted kept saying, "Cut it out Sid people are staring they have the wrong guys, you'll see." When they arrived at the local police station, even the Sheriff's deputy, Flann, was sitting handcuffed to a chair. Then Mr. Cool Ted Heims started shaking and yelling, "I want an Attorney!"

CHAPTER 29

JUDGE CALDER AND JULIE were driving home to Laura's, Julie hiccupping a few brief sobs, like strangled sounds coming from her throat. The Judge handed her a bottle of water, clearing his throat, he said, "I guess you know your Dad was my best friend and I don't know what I'm going to do without him. I lost my Dad a few years ago and it was the most lonesome feeling I have ever had, I try to remember the good times we had together. In the next few days you might hear some things about your Dad you don't like, but always remember how much he loved you. He was so proud of you." Julie covered her eyes, "He was mad at me I just can't live with that.!"

The Judge said, "You mean because of this boy you met on Sunday, forget about that, Brian never liked counselors in any shape or form. He thought they were too wishy-washy, always feeling sorry for clients. He felt the same way about psychiatrists. He thought they were phony, he always said action not talking kept most people going and you have to admit Julie, your Dad saw some of the worst of the human race. He believed firmly that no amount of counseling would help the criminal element. What I will tell you though, is your Dad admired, how stubborn you are, he often said, no one would dare bully my kid, not because of who I am, but because she refuses to accept anything, if she thinks it's wrong. He would proudly tell everyone "She don't take shit from anyone not even me!" Julie said, "Thank you that means a lot to me, I just can't believe he's dead and I'll never see him again." The Judge, "You have memories left and that's what is important, just make sure, you remember the good stuff."

When they drove up to Laura's, Julie ran to her mother's arms. Doug Fresman was pacing back and forth in the front room; nervous, "He said, "Judge can we talk outside." Megan was sitting on the deck still smoking, when they came out. The three of them looked more than grim, more like scared to death.

Laura, Julie and Nina were all holding each other, talking all at once, nothing made sense except Brian was dead. Doug Fresman and the Judge came in the house and stood facing the three women, Megan standing behind them. Doug said, "Laura we need the key for the green house room." She said, "Oh, Doug that rings into the Sheriff's office, I'd have to call them first, what in the world would you want from there anyway?" "Well," nervous he said, "We-ah—had them turn the switch off; clearing his throat, you see Brian kept some cash in there he didn't report to the IRS, I think we should get it out, of course they will be-ah-looking at everything. The three women looked at him like he was insane.

The Judge said, "Get the key—right now!" Laura jumped up from her chair, "What's wrong with you two or should I say three, what in the Hell is going on I really need to hear this right now?" Doug shaking, "Please its important Laura!" Julie a dazed look on her face, "What do you mean hidden money; Mom do you know about this?" Laura sat down, "Your Dad's been—well—acting funny—I don't know—he goes in the green house room, when he thinks I'm not home. One day I came home early from my book club and he came out of the green house with a box and a damn gun, for a minute he didn't seem to recognize me, it was the strangest thing; I don't know—glaring—then he pushed past me—got in the car and drove off. Every time I think of that day; well I was never afraid of your father before, but I am ashamed to admit, I was after that incident." She got up and handed Doug the key from her china cupboard. Doug and the Judge hurried out-Megan was already at the greenhouse talking on her cell phone. All three disappeared into the greenhouse. Nina watching out the window turned to Laura and Julie with a frown on her face, "What the Hell—Laura—is going on? I didn't tell you before, but I think Doug is going crazy, sometimes he acts—I don't know—like sneaky and I've caught him lying—He's been up to something no good I can tell. I just pretend like everything is all right, but it's not!"

Julie went out on the deck, first Doug, red faced, puffing, carried a briefcase and a suitcase to his car. Megan, high heels clicking, in a hurry carrying a file box with a strong box on top. Julie called out, "I think maybe you should be showing Mom and I what's in the boxes."

The look Megan gave her was pure hate. Julie grabbed her arm, "I mean it—just stop—I want to see what you have there!" Judge Calder came out then and in a—court room voice-, "JULIE BACK IN THE HOUSE, MIND YOUR OWN BUSINESS, YOU DON'T NEED OR EVEN WANT TO KNOW ANYTHING ABOUT THIS!" Julie came charging at him "Give me that box right now; eyes on fire, stop all of you. You are going to tell me what's going on here!" Suddenly, it's as if they dropped from the sky, men dressed in black vests were everywhere, surrounding Julie and the others. Julie ran screaming for her mother to the house, Laura came running only to skid to a halt by a man holding a piece of paper in his hand, a search warrant, she said, "For God's sake will someone please tell me what's going on, dear God I've just lost my husband and everyone I know is acting crazy, that's when she looked up at the man with the search warrant—it was Pete Kall—she stood with her mouth open. Pete Kall apologizing "I'm so sorry, believe me, Mrs. Denning, but we have a warrant to search your property and—ah—God help me—looking up-to detain you for questioning he finally looked her in the face. Laura still stunned, "Pete why—what—are you doing here?""I'm an FBI agent and believe me after getting to know you, well this is—the hardest thing I have ever done. I wish I didn't have to do this, but it's unfortunately my job." Two other men stood in her kitchen behind him. "Laura started screaming, "You were a spy . . . or what?" "Yes!" "My God, for what reason? What are you looking for?" Confused she looked at Julie and Nina, "Am I hallucinating, putting her hands over her ears, help me someone I think I'm going nuts like everyone else here!" Pete rushed to her throwing his arms around her . . . . please let me explain." Laura, white face, now flushed—slapped him as hard as she could." Get away from me—spying on me—Dear God!" Pete backed off, hands out, "I took the liberty of calling your brother, he's on his way, he is an attorney; right—I have filled him in—that much I stuck my neck out for you. I am so sorry for what you have to face in the next few days, I wish I could help you, but at this time I have to remain impartial. I hope you in time will forgive me. Head down he went to Brian's den where the officers were going through files and boxing up the computer and office files. Another man came up to Laura and showed her identification—IRS—he said hopefully we'll be out of your way in a short time.

Horrified, confused, numb, Julie, Nina and Laura watched as the men in black put handcuffs on Doug Fresman, Judge Calder and Megan, they said "You are under arrest for operating a crystal meth laboratory—accessories to murder—laundering illegal drug money, the list went on and on!"

Laura stood frozen, Nina huddled on the couch. Julie sat down with her head between her knees, then she heard Uncle Dave's voice. Thank God she thought I can't take anymore of this. Laura held on to the edge of the couch by Nina, slowly she slid to the floor, she then curled up in a ball, hiding her face. Her brother sat on the floor beside her and said, "Remember what Ma always used to say, "This too shall pass." You need to remember that every day until we can get this mess cleared up, for one thing, he looked at all three women—you had better be damn grateful the feds feel none of you know what this is all about and that you had no part in it, there's going to be some serious jail time for the people involved in these charges." By the time Dave got done explaining to the three stunned women, that Brian, Doug, the Judge and Megan were involved in a drug ring, and a MURDER, they were like rag dolls. He said, "There are millions of dollars involved, some of it hidden in a corporation—DCF—and a lot of cash in your own panic room in the green house. Brian being the asshole he was—and yes I don't say that lightly—I mean it . . . kept precise records of everything hidden there. You will be questioned, but they have all ready kind of . . . decided the three of you knew nothing about this. Although it's hard for me to believe as sharp as you are—Julie—you didn't figure it out—all the fancy things and this magnificent house, oh well Brian could make anybody believe him, he used to fool me until I realized or instinct told me something was off about all this money. Julie whispered, but we made it from the guest ranch. No," You didn't that's what he told everyone it's a lie.

The federal people were scheduled—today—to arrest everyone involved, with this simultaneous, this morning. Brian's death changed all that, they have—almost—everybody in custody now. And if your wondering, "Did I know about this, before today? I knew there was an investigation being done, but I had not a clue, that Brian was in this deep, Doug Fresman I wouldn't trust to be honest on anything in this mess, I feel the same about Calder, their vicious men, sorry Nina,

I think you—know—I'm right. Laura and Julie I can only advise you legally,

Oh, God, I wish you didn't have to go through this. I am staying right here until this is over, I hope you know how much I love both of you." Laura and Julie beyond words nodded their heads "Yes." Dave trying to be quiet, making hand gestures, like let's not talk about this until the feds are gone, finally seeing the misery and questions in the women's eyes, he said, "Ah, Laura is there someplace we could go that's private." Laura stood up still holding Julie, Nina on her other arm, "I guess we could go out to the garden shed, I put a table and chairs in there, she flushed—so Pete and I could have lunch out there, ah, I guess we need to know the worst, help me bring the coffee and rolls out and we will just listen Dave, and I thank you for always being there for me."

Once they had hot coffee in front of them even though even Dave was shaking it seemed to bolster their spirits enough to face the truth. Dave started talking, "About six months ago, perfect crystal meth started showing up in saddles in—get this—South America. The three women sat looking at him like so, well the meth was traced back to the Pringles in South Dakota, the DEA sent an agent here or rather out by the Pringles ranch, well he ended up buying a ranch— Burton Knight— Laura and Julie gasped, "We met him Saturday night at Vanna's, they looked at each other, Oh My God, Vanna, Laura said, "She will go completely nuts, Dave you need to explain all this to her too." Julie said "She's coming here as soon as they did chores, oh please just tell us, I feel so vulnerable, not knowing anything." "Well, it seems Brian and Doug and Calder picked a few kids every year from Middleborg pharmacy students to make meth in some kind of perfect set up in an underground lab, out on the prairie, that part I don't know yet, where for sure it is. It seems Brian made a deal with some local Pharmacist to supply him with the ingredients.

Apparently the Danford's at the Guest Ranch were in on this too, because they were arrested this morning, they were witnesses for the kids that worked in this lab, testifying that on Spring Break the kids stayed at the Guest Ranch. Next, I guess is this Joel Moss, who tells a whole lot of people his story after he gets picked up for selling meth, only he keeps quiet as to where this secret lab is because he got a short prison sentence and he tells his prison counselor, Blake Denton and his mother that he is going to find this lab and prove it really exists." Julie, Laura and Nina by now are going, "He came here and had dinner with us Sunday, he told us he was trying to find this boy because he jumped parole and was missing," Julie said, "Joel Moss?" Dave said, "Yep, that's the name, okay so this Blake Denton hooks up with some attorney in Rapid City, who is defending another boy, Todd Ames who tells the same story as Joel except he don't know where this lab is because they always taken there in the dark, so he turns himself in to Brian, Doug convinces him to serve a short prison sentence and then they will clear his record, this Todd goes along with this. Now, this is the part I just can't get my mind to accept and your all going to have a fit, but this Todd is the prisoner Brian was driving this morning and this kid insists Brian tried to shoot him and blew up the van instead, the kid—Dave holds up his hand here—I know, let me finish okay? . . . . This kid ends up on the O'Malley ranch burned and bloody and tries to hold Lorinda and her Mom hostage, somehow this Burton Knight gets there and they get the kid calmed down and get a Medivac helicopter to take him out. In the meantime, the feds found all kind of meth making stuff scattered around Brian's van, they think he delivered the stuff to the secret lab and somehow got the kids to make it and then the Pringles sold it all over." Nina biting her nails, "Then what did Doug do, do you know?" Doug was the enforcer keeping all the people in line that worked for this drug ring, also he helped launder the cash by using a dummy corporation, called DCF. Calder and Megan helped set up the deal in the beginning, the Judge supplied the money for the equipment and Megan kept the books.

Dave running his hands through his hair, "I saved some bad news until last because right now you won't care about this, but in a few weeks, ah, you will! The feds are going to freeze your assets. They more than likely will take what cash there is and all of Brian's fancy . . . what do you call them Laura . . . . his big boy toys, well they will get anything of his that's got any monetary value. The house Laura I might be able to save and Julie's college money, I think, no I'm pretty sure I can get Brian's life insurance for you, it was a lot, and this Pete Kall all ready made some kind of deal where you can keep the money that Brian made as Sheriff and maybe some health benefits. You're going to have to be careful with money is what I'm telling you. Please Laura, don't piss off this Pete Kall—he has really tried to help, . . . Okay." Laura by now, drained, "How long, choking, how long, how many years was Brian running a meth lab??" Dave said, "We think it was all set up about three years ago." Nina still biting her nails, "Dave if I give you a dollar, can you represent just me?." "Yes, I think you know I would not help Doug in anyway, give me a dollar, apparently you have something to tell me . . . right?" Nina went on, "Last week and I'm not lying, I just found out we own the villa in Italy, we supposedly rented all these years, I started kind of paying attention to the money, I . . . Dear God . . . this is hard to tell all of you . . . I thought Brian, Doug and Calder were taking kickbacks from criminals or blackmailing somebody, they let slip through the legal system. I have been crazy trying to figure out what to do, who to tell." Julie after a long silence, in a little girl voice, "Uncle Dave did Daddy murder somebody?" Dave said, "Let's just say your Dad saved us all a lot of grief by blowing himself up, I'm sorry I should not have said that!" Julie whispered again, "I heard them say to Doug, accessory to a murder!" Dave said, "No, his arrest warrant said accessory to the murder of Joel Moss." Julie fainted.

CHAPTER 30

LORINDA AND MOLLY WERE both trying to give Marge Moss some comfort; they asked Marge all about her son and what she did for work. Jim Ball and Blake kept going from window to window looking out. Molly told them, "It's highly unlikely the Pringles would come to her for help, they were never close friends." Blake asked Lorinda if he could borrow her cell phone as Burton had asked him to keep his free until whatever Burt was doing was over. Lorinda said, "Sure and I guess Mom maybe you had better call Dad, I hate this, but my guess is we are going to need him, if nothing else to do Burt's chores." Molly got right on the phone, first she tried to tell Frank what all had happened, then she handed the phone to Lorinda, "Dad wants to talk to you," Frank told Lorinda that she could probably start Burt's tractor better than the one she was using at home, it was a lot bigger and easier to handle, he went on, "You probably will need to give his cows a couple of bales, the grass is pretty short this time of year, just roll it out like you do at home. Now tell me again what your mother just told me because I finally figured out how to put this damn phone on speaker, so Tom can hear all this plus I don't think I took in all your Mom had to say, for one thing I'm sorry as hell, you and your mother had to go through this alone, I don't need to go hunting ever again!" "Whoa, Lorinda said, "We are fine, at the present time we have a prison counselor and a Sheriff staying with us. Do not drive too fast home, but I will admit we do need you and could Tom come on home with you, my whole world here seems to be falling apart and I want my brother, Tom are you listening?"

In the mean time Blake was on the phone with Will and Beth States, they were upset what had all happened to innocent people, but admitted, they were thrilled that their investigation had helped shut down a meth lab, they said some big wheel in charge of the DEA (Sam

Davis) had called and told them, and apologized for stonewalling Beth, when she contacted them, but without her research, they would not have caught all the people involved. Will said Beth was tickled pink, when she seen on T.V. the nasty snot kid was arrested." Blake said, "It's on T.V. all ready, holy cow!" When he hung up he said, Quick turn on the T.V., it's on there, I mean some of the arrests. They all stood around the T.V., when Marge started yelling, "Yes, Oh, ha, ha, look at that smart ass Ted Heim, is he crying? Oh my God I never thought I would see this day, I know it's mean to be glad some other young kid is in trouble, but if you only knew what a cocky, nasty young man he is well I'm glad he's in trouble." Jim said, "Ah, I'm not trying to be bossy but how about calling your Dad before he sees this on T.V., not that he deserves it, but the shock that he was wrong might—ah—just kill him." Marge smiled, "Your right, I'll call my brother and have him go to Dad's and maybe I'll call him myself, well just to gloat, except I'm so kind of mixed up right now, I would rather have Joel alive, than all this revenge.

They all heard about the third helicopter going over the house and Lorinda said, "I am really getting worried about the cattle and horses, they're are kind of crowding up to the fence by the barn—hungry all eeady—and I'm afraid, these helicopters are going to scare them through the fence, then I will have an immediate problem that's real, not that someeone may come after us." They all started looking out the windows, Lorinda, nervous, "Blake, can you call Burt and tell him I can't wait much longer to feed?"

Perfect timing, Blake's cell phone rang, it was Burt, "Put this on Speaker. Is Jim still there? "Yep", from Jim. "Blake, you were right the Pringle's went home all right—not to change clothes though—they were all four in a big Winnebego heading down their driveway. Thank God you told me you suspected, they were nervous or scared or something, we might have had to arrest them taking a chance on other people being in the way. Because it was out in the middle of nowhere, they had no place to run, so we arrested them without incident. You would not believe what all was in that camper. Please can you stay there, a little longer; our big take down is yet to come." Blake said, "Lorinda is getting kinda worried about the chores, and what's with all the helicopters." Burt said "Give us another hour and we will have this operation mopped up, with any luck, without any one getting hurt." Blake shrugged when he hung up,

"I still don't know who, what or where this lab is and who is going to be arrested yet, I thought after the Pringle's it would be over. He won't tell me what this stupid Turtle Mountain or hill or whatever has to do with all this." Lorinda and Molly looked at each other like, "No, it can't be." Blake looking at them said, "What tell me!" Both looked grim, "Turtle Mountain is right across the bluff from Dale and Vanna Schultz's place, their place sits on one hill and then a gully and then . . . ah . . . Turtle Hill—every time this Turtle has been mentioned, we both are holding our breaths, praying, it's not what we think. Vanna has a root cellar in the hill side, that overlooks the turtle, both sat down by the table, I know we are both thinking the same thing, what if Vanna is involved somehow—ah—the first thing Frank said after we told him this story was, "This sounds like something Vanna would think up, she would steal the gold out of her dead mother's teeth, if she thought she would get by with it." Lorinda almost crying now, "I couldn't believe when Dad said that to me, I was shocked and yet some part of me knows he just might be right." "Oh, I don't think it's her, Blake said, I mean she's kind of a big shot in this part of the country right?" "Yes, your right Blake, she is a wonderful person, we just can't put the location out of our heads and Brian was well respected too.

CHAPTER 31

DALE SCHULTZ CALLED HIS hired man . . . Barney . . . on the cell phone."
Barney where are you? I don't know if you heard yet, that Vanna's brother
had an accident this morning . . . ah . . . well, he's dead." Barney said,
"Yes he had heard and didn't know quite what to do, so he kind of just
stayed out of the way. He said, "He was feeding the calves they had just
weaned and they were still doing a lot of bawling, but were starting to
eat." Dale answered back with, "Are the cows starting to calm down, I
don't want them breaking down any gates, and getting to those calves."
"No," Barney laughed, "They seemed to be more interested in hay this
morning than their babies, boy, after three days of bellowing, I needed
a rest from all the noise." Dale said, "Well, I guess we are on our way
up to Laura now and I need some things from town. Could you go in
and pick them up, I'll call in an order to the hardware store and charge
dinner to us at Al's." "Well" Barney said, "I'm not quite done with
chores, I'll go when I get done." Dale said, "Go now and have an early
dinner before the Diner fills up you can always finish up when you get
home."

As Barney was driving off he thought 'Why is Vanna using a five
gallon pail to water flowers around the house for crying out loud she
has enough hose to go around the world." Sam Davis didn't catch on
either in his helicopter flying over the ranch, if he had been a rancher,
he would have caught on when he seen Dale go open the big corral
gates and start chasing newly weaned calves out to the pasture to their
weary mother's. At first the calves couldn't believe they were being
turned out, than one after another, until ten at a time were trying to
go through the gate. Their Mama's were just as shocked, they all ran
as fast as they could away from the ranch as Dale waved and shouted,
running at them. Daleran for all he was worth for the garage, backing

a brand new Lincoln car out, he ran to help Vanna with her third can of—diesel fuel.

The car running sitting by the house kind of worried Sam Davis from his sky view, but it still looked like two people driving somewhere for a visit until he trained binoculars on the car, it was full of suit cases and what looked like metal storage containers. Then he saw them both running down the hill from the house pouring, oh, oh fuel, No, he thought "What the Hell!"

Barney couldn't believe his eyes when he came over the hill from the Schultz place, there was every kind of Law Enforcement vehicle, sitting all along the road, even a SWAT van; Lordy, Lordy, he thought, "What has Miss Vanna done now?" He slammed on the brakes, in front of him stood Burt Knight with a badge in his hand. Barney's eyes got huge, Burt walked up to him and said, "Barney we need to talk. Climb in this SUV with me." There were two other very stern-looking black vested men sitting in what Barney just knew was an FBI outfit, it looked like, what he had seen on those T.V. cop shows." Barney said, "You know I always thought there was something different about you, can you tell me what in the world your doing standing in the middle of the road and who the hell are you really?" Burt told him as quick as possible why they were here and what was going to happen. Barney took a chew of tobacco out of his pocket, "I'm not supposed to know, but I do know ain't any of my business, I mind my own business, see, but yeah I know they do something in that old root cellar, they had some crew out here a few years ago fix it all up and you can bet I never got to see what they were working on." "How much trouble can you make for me for just guessing, not knowing for sure?" Burt said "First, we are going to want to know, what you think goes on here."

"Well I don't know for sure, but I guessed maybe they were hiding like bad guys or something, like the mafia or something like that. "Burt, had to laugh, but was relieved, that Barney did seem innocent."

Dale and Vanna ran to the car. Then Barney said, "Yeah and them big shot friends of Dennings, were out here all the time, while they were fixing up that cave or whatever it is, you know them, that States Attorney and some big wig like a Judge or something, you woulda thought that Judge owned the place like he acted."

Vanna ran to the car getting in the driver's seat, while Dale lit what looked like a blow torch to Sam. "Oh my God he yelled, they're going to blow the lab in fact the whole place, I didn't catch on in time. Get out of there all of you, . . . Move! . . . that bitch was pouring fuel all over the place."

Dale threw the blow torch on the path going down the hill, fire erupted going two directions, popping and crackling flames all ready jumping up the wind was blowing fire everywhere. Vanna gunned the big powerful engine, racing down the driveway, neither her or Dale said a word to each other.

Over their radio's came a screaming yelling, cussing Boss, "What the bleep, bleep, could go wrong."

Enforcement vehicles were spinning their wheels trying to get out of the way, it was like a race car track, nearly colliding with each other as they tried to get below another hill to take cover. Right behind them came Vanna, eyes wild, hair sticking out like a mad woman, Dale holding on for dear life, she was flying over bumps, the car fishtailing all over the road driving like a race car driver.

Everyone got down the hill and out of their vehicles, on the ground—except Burt's SUV, when the explosion hit . . . . it was like an earthquake, Knight's outfit tipped on its side, windshield blown out. They were all rocking back and forth like waves hitting a boat. The SWAT team managed to run to Burt, his men and Barney. Burt swore up a blue streak, as he climbed out a window on the side, they pulled Barney out next, he went, "First off, what the hell was that, second, I think I swallowed my chew, and third, it you smell something I think I shit my pants." Burt a few cuts and bruises, one of his men held his arm, a grimace on his face, he said, "Go on without me I'll catch a ride down to an ambulance I think I have a broken arm." Burt swore some more. His supervisor came over the radio, "Burt answer me are you all right and are your men all right?" "We are shook up is all and I think, Boyd broke his arm, he's the worst hurt." Sam Davis plain roared over the radio, "I've all ready called the air force base and the Forest Service to get chemical plane's out here, or this whole damn country will burn up, they're on their way, how many fire trucks do we have? There's about five of us was the answer, but we are lucky the Indian firefighter's just happen to be at a fire, south of here, they're on the way here." Sam Davis, "This was supposed to be a simple arrest, all carefully planned out!" Why the Hell would Denning pick today to blow himself up and put the rest of the bunch on the run—shit—I know—that's life?"

Sam went on, "Does anyone have a tire popper and who's down below that third hill?" A young patrolman came on, "Sir, there's three cars down here and we have all ready put out a popper, she's coming over these hill now, we are going to stop her one way or another!" Sam said, "If you have to, shoot her, shoot the car first, but don't let her get away!"

At the very top of the third hill from the ranch, Vanna seen she was surrounded, she screeched to a halt, dust flying, when the air cleared they could see her and Dale standing with their hands in the air. Using a blow horn the SWAT Team drove up to them, "Vanna Schultz, you are under arrest for the murder of Joel Moss!" Fast, just a blur, Dale still standing—she jumped in the still running car, gunning the motor, she smashed through a ditch—then a barbed wire fence, then picking up speed, she literally flew the car through the air over a cliff.

Men with guns stood stock still for a few minutes, finally someone put handcuffs on a stunned—Dale. "You are under arrest for maintaining a Methamphetamine Lab on your property and an accessory to murder, there are other charges pending."

Several men climbed down to the car, standing straight up and down on its hood. Vanna was hanging out the windshield . . . . dead.

Fire trucks were coming from every direction and a chemical plane was dropping all ready. Sam had told them to let the buildings burn just contain the fire around the ranch, so no one else would be burned out.

Burton Knight sat on the ground—it's over—now, we find that poor boy's body. Little did he know there would be more than one body buried there.

CHAPTER 32

Lorinda, Molly, Blake, Jim and Marge, were watching the news as the reporter kept showing all kinds of people going in and out of the Police Headquarters in Rapid City, Molly said, "They must have moved everyone there because it's a lot bigger place, covering her eyes, "Is that Doug Fresman in handcuffs, I can't look, Lorinda is it?" Lorinda watched as Doug was led into the building, "Tired she said, "Who else do you think could be involved in making drugs, for God's sake,—Why.?" "Money was the answer each one of them knew in their mind." Jim turned to Marge, "I think I see that Deputy Flann from this morning, right behind . . . . What in the world? . . . . behind Judge Calder. He was about the toughest Judge especially on drug dealers or even kids that used. How can he hold his head up like that and how is he involved?"

Suddenly a large boom was heard and the house shook, they could hear one explosion after another, as they all ran outside, a huge cloud of smoke rose to the east, in amazement, like a silent movie, they watched some of the cows break down a gate and run toward the house, other's bawling ran further out in the pasture. The five of them had no time to wonder what happened, they were all chasing cows, trying to herd the scared animals back to safety. Blake's cell phone rang from his shirt pocket, it was Burt Knight, "Is everyone all right?" "Yes, what was that an explosion or what?" Burt said, "I can't talk now, I need Lorinda or you or someone to bring Frank's big tractor from the machine shed, we have a big fire and we need it to dig a fire break by a gravel road, we hope to stop the fire, from going any farther." Jim yelled, "I can run the tractor over there if it's safe to leave now." Burt desperate, "Come, nothing is safe from the fire but the S.O.B.'s that started this mess are under control, I will call later and explain all I know." Jim and Lorinda ran for the shed, Jim had the big tractor running and was soon down the road toward what Molly said "She thought had to be the Schultz place."

Marge, Blake, Lorinda ran after the livestock, while Molly held open the gate. Molly went to the house to make dinner, while the other three finished Lorinda's chores. Marge said, "There's nothing like some good old exercise to make a person feel better, I know I do." Everyone agreed.

Blake's cell phone rang as they got back to the house, "It was Burt, "Listening Blake's face turned white, "He said I have to sit down, handing the phone to Lorinda," Burt said, "I think the fire is confined, but please watch it if it gets any closer, please go over to my place, will you promise me!" "Yes." "Blake will fill you in on what happened, God, how I wish I could come personally, but I have my hands full right now. Jim will be back soon with the tractor wait until he can tell Marge Moss about her son and what happened here today. I know you thought a lot of Vanna Schultz and Dale, the underground Lab was right below their house under everyone's nose . . . . all this time . . . and it gets worse. Lorinda listen carefully, ah, We have a satellite picture, showing plain as day Vanna shooting Joel Moss, I know this is hard to believe, but-ah—she might have killed someone else too." "Lorinda handed the phone to Blake, stunned she kept shaking her head. Jim walked in just then dirty and smoky smelling, "My God what a mess, it's about over burning on the prairie, but the buildings will smolder for days. Marge, you might need to sit down, ... okay . . . . ah . . . it looks like Brian Denning's sister, Vanna Schultz, shot and killed Joel . . . . wiping his eyes . . . then they buried him on their ranch I guess he found out too much, we don't know, for sure. The Fed's now think she was the main instigator, of this meth lab, and well, it sounds like she was the brains behind all the money, distribution and finding people who loved money more than human life. I know you worshiped her . . . Lorinda . . . but she was . . . well, insane I think . . . . She proceeded to spread diesel fuel all around her house and made a trail to the meth lab, she knew how dangerous the chemicals are for meth, of course it blew sky high. Then she . . . ah . . . drove her and her husband off the ranch just before it blew, what she didn't expect was to be met by about a hundred law personnel waiting for her, the one decent thing she did was let her poor husband out of the car and then drove off a cliff . . . . she's dead . . . and

I'M GLAD . . . sorry . . . Lorinda and Molly. Blake defensive, "Jim how do they know for sure it was Vanna who shot Joel, I mean she had lots of help, even her husband is guilty as hell, he must have helped her?" Jim said, "I understand they enhanced a satellite image and she is the one pulling the trigger on a shot gun and yes, her husband, is just as guilty or maybe worse, he allowed all this to go on, and he covered up her messes."

Lorinda could not stop crying, sobs wracked her body. Molly rushed to her and gathered her in her arms. Lorinda sat down at the table, hands over her ears, Molly's arms around her shoulder's, she looked up at her mother, "Mom, if a bearded man walked in the door and said, "I'm Jesus Christ, the end of the world has come; . . . . Come with me . . . I'd grab his hand and go!"

Marge finally spoke up, "I'm sorry, but I have no tears left, I must have cried a bucket full by now! You mean this evil woman shot my son! WHY??? Dear God help me get through this. My son died because a lot of people wanted to be rich . . . . including him. Truly money . . . is . . . the root of all evil!" In the quiet that followed, Blake's cell phone rang yet again, it was Julie, "Blake I have something to tell you . . . . and . . . . if you never want to see me again . . . . I will understand . . . . you see my . . . . !" "Stop," from Blake "Julie, just stop right there, I know everything about your Dad, Doug and the Judge . . . ah . . . everything!" "Shocked, choking, "How could you know all ready . . . How?" Blake, "Last night we met Burton Knight and Lorinda at the truck stop." "Yes, that seems like a lifetime ago!" Well Julie, I happened to know Burt was a D.E.A. big shot and I couldn't figure out why he was pretending to . . . . NOT . . . know me. I have met him several times. After I went back to my motel, he called me. We had said we were going to your Aunt Vanna's this morning and he begged me to keep you from there. When I insisted he tell me why; he said they were arresting your Dad and Aunt at the ranch, this morning, it was a sting operation, a whole lot of people were involved in making and selling crystal meth. He thought if he told me, I would tell . . . . you. It's the hardest thing I have ever done, is to lie to you!" She said, "Why, Aunt Vanna . . . what in God's name does she have to do with all this?" That stopped Blake cold, heart beating fast, "Look, love of my life, my soul mate. I am coming to you right now . . . whether . . . you . . . or your family want me or not!" Blake ran to his car; then ran back hugging everyone saying, "She doesn't know about Vanna, yet, I have to be with her!"

Molly looked at the clock, in surprise, she said "It's only twelve o'clock for goodness sake, this is the longest day I can ever remember, let's eat. I made roast beef sandwiches and potato salad for lunch. She started putting all kinds of things on the table, everyone started to laugh, this is a lunch it looks like a buffet." "Lorinda said, "Mom knows how to make us all feel better . . . food . . . and it works, I feel better all ready."

After they ate, Lorinda asked Jim, "If he would drive her car over to look at the Schultz place, she told all of them, we might as well get it over with, I don't know what's worse for me, Vanna being crazy or that beautiful house burned and gone forever." Molly said, "Ah . . . maybe Marge don't want to see . . . well . . . anyway we can go later." "Marge protested, "I want to see this place, my son did wrong, I taught him from the time he was little that, we all have to pay a price if we make a mistake or lie about something, what's not fair, that he had to pay with his life. He had some of his Dad's ways or maybe my Dad's I don't know, but money meant way too much to him. I blame myself for the fact I could not get a good job, with only a high school education, so we had to watch every penny after his Dad died. My Dad as you might have guessed from Jim and I talking is a . . . well . . . skin flint, all he cares about is his piles of money. Joel really resented his Grandfather for not helping us. I think Joel did something illegal, just to show the old man he could make money too. I don't know, what makes a kid go bad, I tried, but it wasn't good enough I guess." Jim and the others told her in no uncertain terms, not to feel guilty, she was a good mother and Joel worshipped her. Jim said, "Remember what Blake told you. Joel had a lot of respect for you."

When they all got in Lorinda's fancy little sport car, Jim went, "Wow, Holy Cow, this is some car!" Lorinda told him, "You can put the top down if you want, the way I look it doesn't matter if my hair gets anymore messed up." Lorinda insisted Jim and Marge get in the front, off they went, Jim turned to Marge, "I need something like this to drive, it makes me feel . . . well . . . important." They all laughed, then Molly said, "Her Grandma made her buy it!" Lorinda biting a fingernail, "Mom, I feel kind of funny about us telling Burt how I spend too much money because of Grandma. I got to thinking about him asking so many questions about how often Dale and Vanna visited me. I am uncomfortable. Have you or Dad . . . ah . . . ever told him about my past, I mean it could look bad to somebody that don't know me? Molly said, "I was afraid you were going to think of that and absolutely we never told him or anyone else for that matter. Actually you have never told us, but just a few things and we have respected you and Seth's silence on . . . ah . . . Ken."

There were still several police vehicles on the road toward the Schultz place, they passed what looked like a wrecker pulling something up a hill. Jim sober, "That's where she drove off, the front of the car, was like buried in the dirt down there. Don't look . . . okay?" When they got to the last hill overlooking the ranch, Lorinda gasped, so did Molly, there was a huge hole from east of the house right to the house, it looked like from the road that the house had just collapsed in this crater. Two officers were guarding the gate to the ranch, Jim told them they would not go any farther. An old pickup came driving up to them from the smoldering buildings. It was Barney driving and Burt riding. They stopped and got out, so did Jim and his passengers. Barney came right up to Lorinda, who was standing in front of the car by now, looking at Burt as he leaned on Barney's pickup door. Barney said, "Missy Rinda, I just want you to know I had nothing to do with no drug dealing, I know you would hate me forever if I didn't put a stop to that. I am pretty sure I'm going to be in trouble for knowing about the root cellar but I didn't, I swear on a stack of Bibles, know that it was drugs. You and your folks opinions mean a lot to me and I know how you hate drugs after what happened to you!" Lorinda looking toward Burt with fire in her eyes, Well,' "Oh, God" groaned Molly, "Burton Knight my guess is your about to meet the real Lorinda O'Malley and please always remember she goes over being mad, real quick. Ah but only after she blows off!" Lorinda looking at her mother eyes wide, "What the Hell? Your apologizing for me? Listen Mr. D.E.A. agent I got to thinking about some of the questions you asked me, on our supposed pretend date and correct me if I'm wrong, you were only checking me out to see if I was getting in on a little of the drug money." At this she spit on the ground wiping her face with her hands shaking, "You S.O.B. why didn't you just ask?" About then Burt grabbed Barney and crouched down behind him. "Can she see me Barney, does she have a gun?" Everyone laughed except Lorinda, fists clenched," My son and I know what and where Hell is, why because my husband sold drugs, when I found out I got a divorce and turned him in to the authorities, but guess what he got out on bail, AND THEN he came after me with a gun. The so and so finally took an overdose and died leaving Seth and I to be accused of living off drug money and the threats against us from crazy mad people, you have no . . . idea . . . if I even thought my long time friend here was involved in drugs, they would have been in all kinds of trouble, I would have made sure of that. Lorinda put her head down, Marge handed her a kleenex. Burt yelled, "Molly, is it safe to talk now or should I keep hiding? Lorinda does the words, MAKE MY DAY, mean anything to you . . . ah . . . your very important big wig friends tell me in Sioux Falls, you're the person to see if you want help with kids on drugs, I guess you pretty well run the Narcotics Anonymous Group for Families. What they told me was, your husband came after you with a gun and you said (Make My Day and turned your back to him and walked away . . . . ah . . . correct!" Lorinda shading her eyes, looked him in the face, then startled, "What happened to your face and your arm? Hurrying over to him she looked confused at all the cuts and bruises; she reached out a hand and touched his arm where the sleeve had been ripped off of his shirt. Barney slapped his knee, "Honey, you better look off to the west of this hill." Lorinda turning finally saw Burt's SUV crumpled and tipped over windows broken. She put her hand over her mouth, "Oh My God, how bad hurt are you? Broken ribs what and did they disinfect these cuts, Oh, My God. You had better come home with us Mom has enough food to feed an army, Well why didn't you say you were hurt, by now she had her arm around him, looking him over like a little kid. Burt trying not to laugh, "And my Darling, of course, I checked you out, for God's sake I'm a, Cop, that's my job, you were hanging around with some dangerous criminals. What they also told me from the Sioux Falls headquarter . . . get this . . . that the drug dealers were more afraid of you than they were of the cops." Molly said, "I think we had better think a little more about Marge's feelings right now, than your hurt pride, Lorinda." They all looked at Marge, who looked up at the sky and quietly whispered—Where is he?"

Burt limping holding tight to Lorinda's arm, "He's buried straight north from where we are standing—his car too—in a little gully. Do you want to be here when the skid steer or digger gets here?" She shook her head, "No, I think I want to remember the way he looked the day he left home!" Burt putting his arm around her, "This sting operation turned into kind of a disaster, but maybe because Denning blew himself up trying to shoot Todd, well at least his life was spared. Also it would have been hard to prosecute Denning and this Vanna, they both had some powerful friends, so maybe its best what happened. We would have been a lot longer finding this well hidden lab if Joel had not reported it, he gave us the location through you and Blake Denton, from the grave you might say. My guess from all the meth distribution going on, Joel likely saved a lot of lives. I hope that's some comfort to you." Marge quiet, "Thank you, that means a lot to me."

Burt still leaning on Lorinda, "Now what I think should happen here is Lorinda goes home with me and helps me shower and get in some clean sweats and helps me get in my recliner and brings me a cold beer and Molly brings all the army food to my house while Barney does my chores, oh and I forgot I think Lorinda should stay with me for a week or so until I get on my feet." Everyone laughed except Lorinda, whose face turned bright red. Molly said, "I definitely think your right and that's just what's going to happen." Burt holding on to Lorinda, "One thing I'm not kidding about, I think I threw my back out, it hurts like hell. Please, Lorinda go with Barney and me . . . Okay. "I don't know about the shower, but I am pretty sure I can handle everything else your Royal Highness requests! Oh, I forgot Dad will be here tonight and Tom. He said he will run things for you for a while. "Barney, "Molly tell Frank that the Schultz cattle are running loose all over scared to death. I'll try to round them up tomorrow, but I could sure use some help." Molly asked if any of them were hurt. Barney, "I'm not sure, Dale ran them all out to pasture just before they blew the damn place up and the calves are back with the cows, but he did a decent thing there." Burt, not letting go of Lorinda, almost drug her to Barney's pickup. Off they went in a cloud of dust. Burt said, "Barney, which do you like the best, Miss Lorinda the spiked heel city lady, with a slit up her skirt, bare back or the real Lorinda we are seeing today, with the hair standing straight up and the designer chore girl outfit of today?" Barney shaking his head, "Now you're going to get me in trouble, personally, I like that . . . ah fancy dress . . . ah . . . but I guess I'd rather live with the one sitting right here." Burt said, "Me too!" Lorinda looked at both of them disgusted arms crossed, "Well I know I damn well could live without the smell of you two."

CHAPTER 33

IT TOOK BLAKE DENTON a while to get to Julie's, all the time he kept wondering what in the world he was going to say. When he got there, Laura's brother, Dave met him at the door and said, "They had just heard the news about Vanna and Dale." Julie ran to Blake holding on to him like a drowning person. Laura got up and shook his hand, "Blake, I would very much like it if you could go check out of your motel room and if it's possible could you stay with us for a few days. I don't know for sure, but my guess is we are going to have trouble coming at us from every direction, including very angry former prisoner's that Brian arrested." Blake, his arm around Julie said "I have all ready called my boss and I was going to stay whether you wanted me or not. Julie, I would like you to ride with me, we won't be gone long, quite frankly I'm not letting you out of my sight." Laura smiled, "Sorry, you had to meet us under these awful circumstances, but I think you're exactly what we need right now. My brother has a family that needs him too. We are all going to be scrutinized by the public and it's not going to be fun. I will admit at this time, that I am so angry at Brian, I almost hate him, then I wonder how could I love a monster like this, some where's inside of me or I should say some part of me died along with Brian today and I know this sounds crazy, but the part that died, was something that needed to die!" Dave had been on the phone, when he hung up he told Nina, "They were sending someone to escort her home, her house had been searched." Laura said, "Nina is staying here with me, no discussion, she stays here." Nina agreed, but wanted to go home for a change of clothes and she said she wanted to talk to Doug, could she go down to the jail?" Dave called again, "They said she could talk to Doug on the phone, but could not see him, and that they were holding him in a private cell, as they were the Judge, for their safety, it seems there has all ready been threats. "Nina went in another room while she talked to Doug, it was obvious she had been crying, but otherwise seemed calm. Doug told her he deserved whatever sentence he got and that he had them call an attorney, who would look at all the evidence and then decide if he should plead guilty and have it over with, he for one was glad it was over.

Dave had set up an appointment with the funeral home for the following morning. Laura asked, "Do I have to plan Vanna's funeral too, or who . . . ah . . . is she going to do it?" Dave answered, "Sorry, Laura, but Julie's listed as Vanna's only heir, it's going to be awkward, I know, there is no family on Brian's side."

Two young police men knocked on the door, they were to escort Nina, home, and then they were to return and stay at Laura's house, Laura asked, "Did they want to stay in the house or outside?" "They would be outside for two or three nights, but they thanked her for inviting them in."

When Blake and Julie came in the house, Julie said "Mom, there's a big SUV under the oak tree up the driveway, the windows are black. How are we going to tell good guys from bad?" Laura told her they we're going to be under police protection, so boy they were not kidding when they said, "There would be threats. When the two young men returned with Nina, Dave left.

Later in the day Laura's and Nina's minister came, "He admitted, he did not know what to say, but he was going to try." Dave had worried no one would come to offer condolences and he knew Laura needed people around her right now. When he voiced this to Laura, she said, "Dave I've been alone except for Nina and Julie for a long, long time, Brian was never here and if he was he stayed in his office."

Blake stayed awake all night while the three women tried to sleep. At different times during the night, each of them got up restless and visited with Blake, Julie finally came down stairs and slept on a couch curled up to Blake. He was afraid to touch her, she seemed so fragile.

Laura got up early and started coffee and rolls. She took two mugs of coffee out to the police van, two sleepy young men thanked her. She asked, "Who was in the SUV up the hill?" They both looked sheepish, "Ah . . . we are not supposed to tell you . . . ah ma'am." Laura went and got one more mug and marched up the hill, she tapped on the window, "I know it's you Pete, open up and come down to the house for some breakfast, that's an order!" Pete climbed out wrinkled clothes, day old beard and hair sticking up on the back of his head. "I'm sorry, I thought you wouldn't know it was me, the person behind all your trouble, I wanted to make sure you were safe . . . ah . . ." Laura retorted, "Brian Denning made all my trouble, not you, you were just in my line of fire, and I was wrong, come." Pete said, "It won't look right if I'm . . . ah . . . with you, I mean I'm the one digging up evidence against your husband." Laura laughed out loud, "Some husband I had, right, and I couldn't give a shit less what anyone thinks!"

Blake showered and in his dress suit came to sit in the kitchen, "I'm going with you to the funeral home, then I'll sleep."

A knock at the door, Laura answered to see the sheriff from Durant County and his wife at the door with rolls from the bakery and standing behind them was Bob Allard, Blake jumped up and hugged Bob, God, am I glad to see you "Well Bob said, "You're going to see a lot of me from what I hear, I'm going to be your special ladies', guard for a few days, what in the world Pete Kall, well you look like shit, where have you been, I thought you were home sleeping?" Pete tired, "And that's just where I'm going, home to sleep."

CHAPTER 34

LORINDA DID HELP BURT to the shower and then rounded up some clean sweat pants and a tee shirt. When he came out of the bathroom, he could smell coffee brewing. She brought him a fresh cup and helped him to his easy chair he told her where the pain pills were in his dirty shirt. The doctor in the ambulance had told him he might hurt later on.

Jim, Marge and Molly drove up in Jim's pickup, the back seat full of food. Molly called to Barney, who was feeding cattle, to come in and eat. Burt said, "He never tasted anything as good as this meal, the best thing would be if I never had to move any part of my body until these pain pills kicked in, Lorinda can you help me lay down on the floor, all I need is a pillow, my guess is I won't be able to get up, but the floor feels better than a chair." "Molly, Marge and Lorinda all hovered around Burt as he laid flat on the floor. Jim had went out to help Barney finish up chores. When Jim came in he said, "Lorinda, I'll go help you now and then I think we'll head for home." Lorinda, "Thank you can you go right now, it takes some times just to feed the calves, alone. Marge and Molly were already cleaning up Burt's messy kitchen. They said, "We'll gather up something for supper, it looks like there's plenty of food in the deep freeze."

When Jim and Lorinda came back from doing Lorinda's chores there were two or three cars in Burt's yard. In the house was several, what looked like to Lorinda . . . Feds . . . she was right, Burt's boss was there, sitting in a chair talking to Burt as he laid on the floor. Molly and Marge were busy little beavers broiling steaks and washing up baked potatoes for the microwave. Jim got out beer for everyone, including himself. The women stayed in the kitchen when Barney came in to testify, what he knew. They said he was the most help because he had seen all the various people who came and went on the ranch. They were quite sure they had not caught everyone yet especially the ones selling the drugs. Barney said, "The one's he remembered the best were the interior decorator folks, Vanna said, "Were helping her fix up the house, only they carried out more cases than they came in with and then this construction crew, they looked shifty and never seemed to actually do much." Barney was able to recall the names on their vehicles. Sam Davis told him, "He was not surprised at the carrying out cases because, they had found money in everything from cardboard boxes to fancy suitcases. Vanna and Dale had that car stuffed with suitcases of money, the same with the Pringles's."

Frank called Burt's to see if his family were there. Jim drove Molly and Lorinda home. Lorinda and Molly were both talking at the same time telling Frank and Tom about their day. Jim and Marge said, "It was time to go home they had a long drive ahead of them. Marge threw her arms around Lorinda and Molly, "I feel like I've known you forever, please let's keep in touch and could you all come up to Willis sometime, well I mean for Joel's funeral, I want you there if you can come." Lorinda assured her they had already planned on it. Lorinda drove back to Burt's after visiting with her Dad and brother a few more minutes. Burt had got up and went to the bathroom and was back on the floor, all of his co-workers had left he said, "I told them I had my own little maid to care for me." Lorinda tried to sleep on the couch, but Burt kept thrashing around, then moaning, she finally got a pillow and blanket and slept next to him on the floor, holding his hand seemed to help his fidgeting.

The next morning, Burt was some better, so Lorinda decided to go with her Dad and Brother to round up cattle. She got Burt coffee and breakfast and gathered all his fax's, that were so piled up they had covered even the floor of his office. He told her, "Don't worry about me, but ah . . . don't forget I'm a helpless cripple and need food about noon." Lorinda had to laugh, "That's about all the longer I can sit on a horse anymore I'm sure I'll be back by noon.

It was still very warm outside, when Frank, Tom and Lorinda on Daisy rode out, then Barney, and other ranchers, everyone had brought fence fixing, supplies and piled in Barney's old pickup. They all admitted it was fun to play cowboy again. Molly and some of the other wives fixed a huge meal and brought it over to Burt's place, he wanted to be in on all the excitement. Lorinda stayed with Burt for the afternoon and helped him sort through pages of testimonies. She was horrified at all the people involved. Burt told her his boss (Sam Davis) had called and said, "It was the biggest drug bust in the D.E.A.'s history."

CHAPTER 35

JIM AND MARGE GOT home late. Jim spent the night at Marge's guessing the phone call would come and it did. Joel's body had been recovered and was being brought to the Willis Funeral Home. His car was being cleaned up, it looked like all it needed was a new radiator, it actually started up when they pulled it out, the upholstery was ruined, but it still looked pretty good so they said. The funeral home wanted to know if Marge wanted to see Joel. She decided yes she did, Jim talked her out of it as he was told about the lye, so he suggested she wait until the funeral director got him fixed up, she reluctantly agreed.

They were both shocked to find out, two other young men's bodies were found in a car below Joel's, both had been missing for two years. It appeared they too had found the secret lab only to be killed.

CHAPTER 36

BLAKE STAYED WITH JULIE and her mother for the funeral. Brian and Vanna funeral was held together at Brian's church. The church to their surprise was full. Several business people got up and testified that Brian had helped them financially and lent them money if they needed extra. Two former convicts got up and stated that Brian had helped them get back into society and generally cared about them and their families. Vanna's friends said much the same about her, how kind she was to neighborhood children. The local food pantry said, "She was one of their biggest contributors of money and spent many hours helping, box up supplies and sorting clothing.

All in all it was a nice funeral; both Laura and Julie felt better. When they left the church, both sides of the street were lined with police cars. Blake thought, OH, Oh,. Everything went as planned driving to the cemetery, it was on the way back to the church, when a woman holding a carton, that turned out to be eggs; rushed out by the funeral home limousine, and plastered it with eggs, she was grabbed by the police.

A lot of people stayed for lunch after the funeral. Laura asked Lorinda, Molly, and Frank, also Tom to come to the house, later on. She thanked Lorinda for calling everyday and Molly for inviting them to come stay with her for a few days.

Laura's house was full of sad people, but each admitted, they were glad it was over.

Pete Kall stopped for a short visit. He asked to talk privately to Laura he told her, from the paper work they had found, it looked like, she could keep the house and what money that Brian had earned honestly, he was worried it might not be enough for her to live on after awhile. Laura, hugged him, "Oh, Pete, thank you and I'm sorry for reacting the way I did toward you and guess what I all ready got a job at the library, I start next week, they called me. Pete said, AH, ... I'm going to be really busy with all the court cases, but would you mind if I called once in a while . . . ah . . . just to see how you're doing? Laura said, "You had better call me and often, and when are you going to come get those trees finished?" Pete looking around to see if anyone was listening "It's a Damn conflict of interest deal or I would be here every day until we . . . Ah . . . got those trees done." He squeezed Laura's hand and left.

CHAPTER 37

LORINDA STAYED WITH BURT for three days, some of the federal people would drive out and they would work on the cases they were building against the different people involved in the sting. At night Burt would sit with his back to the couch and his feet straight out on the floor, at least he could sit up that way. Lorinda washed curtains bedding and in general gave his house a good cleaning. He decided the night before Joel's funeral, that he had to start getting up and walking because, He was going to that funeral with, Lorinda and her parents. He asked Lorinda to help him to his bed and then see if he could get out of the damn bed by himself, when she got him settled in bed, he grabbed her in a tight grip and pulled her in bed with him. Lorinda, "Even if I did share your bed, wild man, what could you possibly do about it?" Burt meekly admitted she was right. Lorinda knew he was still in terrible pain, so after he fell asleep she went back to the other room to sleep." He was able with her help to get his good suit on and laid in the back seat of Frank's big car with his head on Lorinda's lap all the way to Willis. Actually they had such a good time it was hard to believe they were going to a funeral.

The church at Willis was packed with people, it looked as if the entire town had come to mourn Joel's passing. Joel's classmates got up and sang a song and his former boss gave a speech, all in all it was a beautiful service at the cemetery, Joel's Aunt and his cousins released balloons in the air, saying, "Goodbye Joel." Almost every Federal officer who could get away came to the funeral. Everyone was pleased and really surprised, they came, they all stopped to shake Marge's hand. She said later it made her feel so good. Burt, Lorinda, Molly, Frank and Blake Denton all went to Marge's house afterwards. Marge introduced them as her new best friends; they had shared a terrifying day together, that

111

none of them would forget. Jim never left her side for not even a minute, Blake whispered to Burt, "I bet there is going to be wedding bells in the future, for those two." Burt looked at Blake snorting "And wise guy, when are those bells going to ring for you and that beautiful sweet little gal you found?" Blake blushed, "Damn soon if I have my way!" What about you, Mr. Tough guy, drug agent, rancher, you got time to sweep, Lorinda off her feet or are you too busy, Ha." Burt laughed, "Count on it Sonny Boy, I'm going to make time!"

Driving home Burt said to Frank, "Did you hear your daughters leaving me tomorrow?" Frank said, "Well I'll bet you she will be back, just real soon that is if she wants to keep her fish, I told her I don't have time to take of them and Mom's not going up and down those basement steps." Burt puzzled, "What fish?" Lorinda looking foolish, "Well yesterday when you were busy doing police stuff, Tom and I drove over . . . ah . . . to Vanna's . . . we sorta had to say goodbye to our cherished friend from our childhood. Yeah, I know, she was a vicious criminal in your eyes, but well, we loved her. When we got over to her ranch, we found some Koi fish still alive, I don't have a clue how they could live in that mess, part of the house fell in the pond. The water was coal black, anyway, first two Koi swam up to us and then we found two more, so Tom went home and brought back Dad's old fishing net and we . . . well . . . we managed to catch them, we put them in five gallon pails, in Mom's porch last night, well they were still alive this morning, so, I know this sounds dumb, but Tom went to town while we are gone to buy a plastic stock tank, we're going to put it in the basement at Mom's, I called the pet store for an air filter." Burt said, "You know I can't laugh right now, it hurts too much, but that the damndest thing I have ever heard, what are you going to do with them, keep them in a stock tank forever, Oh God, it hurts to laugh . . . just thinking about your no nonsense brother doing all this, starts me off!" Lorinda defensive, "Tom will do anything I ask him, he loves me, so there!" "Yep," Frank said, "You ought to hear some of the hair brained schemes she has talked her loving brother into, but he still comes back for more, so I guess he must love her!" Molly asked "What time are you and Tom leaving today?" Lorinda held Burt's hand, "I guess when we get home, I'm going to drive as far as his place so I can see Kim and the kids, I guess I'll stay overnight and then leave for home in the morning and darn, darn I don't want to go, but I still have a job and there's still bills to pay, so I have to go." Frank said, "Burt you told her yet?" Lorinda looked down at Burt once again in her lap, "What?" Burt smiling, "Well you will be getting an official invitation soon, but get that slinky black dress and whatever you call those fancy shoes . . . spikes . . . whatever, out in about two weeks your flying with me to Washington D.C . . . to meet the President." "Lorinda actually let out a squeal, "Your getting an award, aren't you tell me, Holy Cow, How I mean how are we getting there?" Burt grinning from ear to ear said, "Well I know it's not quite as exciting as saving fish, but yes, I get an award, and I'm flying to Sioux Falls and then we are flying to D.C. for three whole days. Your Dad is going to keep things at home running smooth, so I can go." In the front seat of the car Frank and Molly held hands; she gave a high five to Frank so Lorinda couldn't see.

Burt told them it would take at least two more months of paperwork and rounding up witnesses, interviews and then he was flying to Texas to official close out his office, he hoped to be back to normal by sometime in December.

Frank had hired a couple of old retired farts, as he called them to help with Burt's ranch.

Tom brought Lorinda's car over to Burt's to pick her up for their long trip home. After Lorinda had ran back to Burt twice to give him a goodbye kiss, Tom hollered, "Enough already for crying out loud, you two act like the end of the world is coming if you don't see each other for what two weeks?"

CHAPTER 38

THE NIGHT BEFORE BLAKE and Julie had to drive back to school and work, Will and Beth States called and invited them for dinner. Julie felt uncomfortable at first, but it was hard not to love this funny wonderful family. It wasn't long before the States children had Julie talked into a game of Old Maid. Beth told them, "To quit monopolizing Julie with video games, they drug out, too." It was wonderful for Julie to see, that people didn't hold her Dad against her.

Blake drove Julie back to school; she tried never to think about her beautiful little red car, burned up at Vanna's. At school Julie ashamed of what her father had done, decided to still keep her head held up. Many classmates surrounded her with love and kindness; many telling her they had skeletons in the closet too. She and Blake spent every weekend together and were talking marriage. They often said to each other, "Something good always comes out of something bad, God does take care of us."

CHAPTER 39

LAURA DENNING SPENT MANY sleepless nights going over and over the terrible events, wondering if she could have stopped any of it. Nina Fresman moved in with her until Doug was sentenced, then Nina planned on getting an apartment close to whatever prison he was sent to. She often said, "I'll stand by my man and then laugh, it sounds dumb, but I still love him."

Every week or so Pete Kall would call from Minneapolis, Laura started looking forward to his calls. They shared all kinds of interests. Pete told her about his divorce. His wife despised the outdoors, so they lived in an apartment in the city. After the divorce, he bought a cabin in the Minnesota woods and lived in an efficiency apartment during the week. He talked often of his upcoming retirement. At Thanksgiving time, he came to visit, he said, "He was in town for upcoming trial dates and would spend Friday and Saturday going over paperwork, but could he take her out for Thanksgiving dinner, she had told him Julie was going to Blake Denton's folks for Thanksgiving. He went on . . . ah . . . I just want to see you." Laura insisted he come to her house for dinner. Dave and his family came over and Nina. They all seemed to enjoy the day and Laura felt like a new person. When Pete left he handed her a card and said, "This is for Christmas, in case he couldn't get away over the holidays." Laura said, "She would be honored if he spent Christmas with her and Julie." He said, "I would really like that, if you truly want me." After he left, Laura opened the card inside was two thousand dollars, she was so shocked, she called him on his cell phone and said, "Pete, I can't take your money, My God, you have been so good to me already." He said, "I have plenty of money and I want you to have it, use it buy some luxury items or spend it on Christmas, but please keep it, it will make me feel better about misleading you."

CHAPTER 40

A LOT OF THE court cases had come up and some chose to plead guilty others demanded jury trials. After questioning Dale Schultz, they got a few answers. Dale pled guilty and was quietly sent away to the Sioux Falls penitentiary. He had refused to go to Brian and Vanna's funerals in handcuffs and shackle's. He would only plead guilty to the meth lab and helping his wife dispose of bodies. He did admit, "That they and the Pringle's knew everything was over when they got a call from Megan Calder warning them. Dale was sentenced to life in prison.

Ted Heim was sentenced to five years. Sid Hess got one year. Some of the other students involved chose jury trials, so they would be drug out for months. Ted Heim's parents were distributing meth so their trial was still to come up. The Danfords lost all their assets, but because of their age, was released on probation and ran the guest ranch for the people who bought it from the federal government.

The Judge and Doug Fresman were sent to a federal prison for life, but were both eligible for parole in 20 years.

Megan Calder turned state's evidence and was released on bail. She promptly disappeared.

Hired man Barney with his testimony led the local police to arrest ten other business people who was attempting to sell the leftover meth. Barney insisted he did not help kill anyone and neither did Dale, but Miss Vanna was crazy, so who knew what all she had done." Barney was released to take care of the Schultz ranch for the government. He moved a trailer house on the ranch and told everybody, "He was a Government employee now!"

Mary and Lester were put on probation and house arrest for three years, so they could take care of their animals and ranch land. The neighbors treated them as if nothing had happened. They and the law felt they had enough to deal with, losing almost all their money and the fact both of their sons would be in jail until they were old men. At least none of the Pringles had known about the deaths, however, everyone including the law wondered about that. There was no evidence found that implicated them in anything, but selling the crystal meth.

Todd Ames recovered from his ordeal. The doctors told him his dip in the cold water tank saved him from worse scarring. He was put on probation for one year and then his record would be cleared. It took him over a year to heal up from the many skin grafts he needed plus a punctured lung and broken collar bone. His parents drove him out to the O'Malley ranch a month after he had been released from the hospital; he wanted them to meet Molly and Lorinda. Lorinda was not there, but he was able to call her and in tongue tied, with a lot of . . . ah's . . . he apologized for what he had done. He wanted his parents to see Daisy the horse. He walked up to Daisy with one of the apples, he had brought a huge box for her, she trotted right up to him, everyone was surprised, but not Todd, he said, "I told you this horse is one of God's angels and I talk about her to a lot of people!" embarrassed he hung his head, "Well, I talk quite a bit about Jesus these days." At Christmas, Todd showed up to see Lorinda and Burt, he had a huge bouquet of flowers for Molly and Lorinda and candy for Burt. He had turned into one fine young man. You can believe him when he says I'm a lot better person today than I was six months ago, yep, good does come from evil sometimes."

CHAPTER 41

BURT AND LORINDA SPENT three days in Washington D.C., an exciting three days. Burt received an award at the White House, it was quite an event. When they landed back in Sioux Falls, Burt hated to leave, they were both tired and both had jobs to go to the next day, so Burt flew out the same day as they got back. He called Lorinda every day. Close to Thanksgiving, he called and asked, "If she could fly to Texas to meet his family for Thanksgiving." Lorinda upset, "Oh how I wish I could, but the Friday after Thanksgiving is my biggest day at work!" Burt said "Well could you get away the first weekend in December, we'll have a family celebration then at my folks."

Lorinda couldn't wait for Burt to get there, she was so excited, she had decorated the yard and every room of the house with Christmas. She went to meet Burt's plane at the Sioux Falls airport, she had made a meal fit for a king, they were not flying out until the next morning for Texas. Burt kept looking at all her Christmas displays, asking, "How the Hell do you find time to do all this and all the baking?" She told him, "She had several small parties every year and it seemed people looked forward to coming over."

They flew to Texas the next morning. Lorinda loved Burt's family on sight. His one daughter kind of hung back, like I'm going to watch you lady, you better be good to my Dad. Lorinda won her over when she offered to babysit her children, while the young couple got to go to a Christmas party. The weekend went by so fast that once again found Lorinda saying goodbye, this time at the airport, because Burt's plane was already there for Rapid City, when they got in. They clung to each other like it was the end of the world to be separated.

The next week Burt called and asked if she could come the week before Christmas and decorate his house, like she had done hers." She said, "If I can convince my boss to let one of the college girls come in and maybe get some extra help temporary, you know what I'm going to do it anyway." "My folks and kids are coming the day before Christmas and leaving the day after and I kind of wanted things nice for them, it's too cold here for people from Texas, but they can handle it for two days. Could your Seth come too?" Lorinda all excited, already planning, "Sure they're coming to my folks for Christmas this year. We do it that way every other year. Oh this will be fun!"

The next day Lorinda got an invitation in the mail from Jim and Marge to their wedding, the Saturday after Christmas, Lorinda called Burt, he had received one too, now Lorinda was really excited, "Oh Burt this Christmas is going to be wonderful." He sighed over the phone, "At least they live close to each other this long distance shit is getting to me and furthermore I don't like being alone out here in the boondocks anymore.'

Lorind thought, well, dummy why don't you ask me to marry you, then ha,

CHAPTER 42

THE DAY BEFORE CHRISTMAS, Laura Denning was trying to be in the Christmas spirit, she wanted to have the same Christmas, as in years past, just as if Brian was still alive. She knew it was going to be hard even though Nina would be here and Julie and Blake were coming tonight. She was busy baking and had decorated the house with all Julie's favorite ornaments.

When the doorbell rang, she thought, I will never get done, so many people had stopped in, she couldn't believe how kind everyone had been and was shocked at how many friends she really had made at the library and others from the various clubs she belonged too. Pete Kall stood at the door, dressed like a movie star or very rich. Shocked she stood looking at him. He asked, "Can I come in for a minute? I have a little gift for all of you and I wanted to see how you're getting along." Laura grabbed his arm "Oh, I'm so glad to see you, what in the world are you doing here? Maybe this Christmas will turn out better than I thought. You come on in and plan and being here for Christmas dinner, no if's or butts about it." As she took his coat he looked around, "My word woman, how do you do all this? This house is beautiful . . . ah . . . I guess I haven't had even a tree for twenty years. Settled at the kitchen table, he started to relax, "What will Julie think of me being here?" Laura laughed, "She thinks you're the best and asks about you all the time."

When Julie and Blake arrived, Julie hugged Pete and told him how much she appreciated what he had done for her and her mom. She said, "Your staying for Christmas, Mom said, You didn't tell her if you were coming or not. I was going to call you tonight and tell you to get your butt over here, it's not that far." Pete looked embarrassed, "I did not want to horn in on your holiday, but I decided this morning . . . I . . . ah . . . just plain wanted to be here."

Christmas Eve brought tears to everyone's eyes as Laura and Julie talked of their past Christmas's with Brian. It seemed to Pete and Blake that the two women had made peace with what happened and were trying to remember only the good times.

Julie jumped up, "Wow, where did the time go? We have to be in church in an hour. Pete you are going to get your things from the motel after church and YOU are staying with us!" Pete protested, Blake said, "You might as well do what she says, I certainly do." Everyone laughed.

The church service was beautiful, everyone carried a candle, when they walked out, a lot of people came up and shook Pete and Blake's hand. Nina, Laura and Julie were overwhelmed with the hugs and little gifts various church members gave them.

True to her word Julie insisted Pete come home with them. He was so pleased, it was obvious by the way his eyes lit up, as they all walked in Laura's warm comfortable home. They had a simple chili and sandwich lunch, then on to the gifts. Laura had Blake open a bottle of wine. Sitting around her beautiful tree, they each got a gift certificate from Pete. The women received clothing store gifts and Blake got a fancy restaurant gift for two. Pete was surprised to open a gift certificate to an expensive sporting goods store. He looked at all of them, "How did you know that I was even coming, much less know that I desperately need a new fishing rod." They all said, "A little bird told us.

The next morning Pete got up early to find Laura busy fixing a huge breakfast. He sat down with a cup of coffee and said, "Laura . . . Ah . . . well could you spent New Year's weekend with me at my cabin in Minnesota? I would meet you in Minneapolis unless the weather turns nasty it's not supposed to, but who knows." Laura put down her bowl of pancake dough and walked up to Pete flour on her hands and gave him a kiss. Pete laughed, "Well I guess that means, Yes."

Blake was going home the day after Christmas and then was returning for Marge Moss and Jim Balls wedding. Julie at first was reluctant to go, but Marge had sent her a special invitation. Julie would spend the week with her mother.

CHAPTER 43

Lorinda talked her boss into letting her off for the week before Christmas. The weather was still nice, just a light covering of snow on the ground. Lorinda had her car completely full of Christmas decorations for outside and inside of Burt's house. She thought, he said he wanted it fixed up like mine, I just hope I can squeeze everything in, not much time.

Arriving first at her folks place, she told them I can't stay long, Burt wants me to fix his place up and fix dinner for his family and all of my family. Molly said, "I have already made some Christmas goodies for you to take over there and I will help with dinner." Molly wiped her eyes, 'It's so good to have you home and looking so happy."

Lorinda honked the car all the way up Burt's driveway, he ran out laughing he hugged her, covering her face with kisses, he stopped dead still when he seen all the stuff in her car. Groaning he said, "How much money did you spend, Oh My God, what is all this stuff?" Lorinda opening the car doors said, "There's lots more in the trunk and a lot of this stuff came here from my house, the rest I went shopping the last minute and clapping her hands, I got just about everything for two hundred dollars except the gifts."

Lorinda had Burt setting up three big lighted deer outside along with a huge snowman and Santa Claus after they were blown up. She waited until the next day to put up the tree and fake evergreen she draped all over the house. When she asked him to bring up bales of straw to the house, he looked at her like she lost her mind. That's when she carefully lifted out her final purchase, a Nativity set, almost life size characters, with real looking animals. She explained part of it was her's from home and part she found half price. The two of them set it all up by the patio door, so it could be seen from outside and from the inside.

Lorinda and Molly went last minute Christmas shopping, they had a ball picking up fun stocking stuffer's and grocery shopping. They met Laura for lunch all three of them trying hard not to remember the past.

Burt was like a little kid on the way to the airport to pick up his family, he said he had never put much effort into Christmas before, his mother always cooked the meal and they opened gifts.

When they drove up to the ranch it was still daylight, but the deer and other yard decorations had Burt's family oohing and aweing, specially his five year old granddaughter, who got out of the car and run from one thing to the next feeling, wonder in her eyes, in the house she insisted on opening the patio door so she could hold Baby Jesus. Burt's mother hugged Lorinda "I have always wanted a daughter like you." Lorinda told her she hoped they didn't overwhelm them, but the entire neighborhood was coming over for a potluck supper that night. Burt's mother, father, son and daughter had come, and they assured Lorinda anything she did was fine with them. The two grandchildren walked from room to room looking at Christmas decorations, their mother's said "Look but don't touch!" Lorinda said, "No, this is all for the kids, they can't hurt a thing unless they try to eat it, don't worry, please."

The neighborhood party was a great success it was a good time for all. Lorinda spent that night after cleaning up with her folks at their house she felt Burt should have time to visit alone with his family plus Seth and Amanda, her children were coming the next day for Christmas Eve.

Lorinda went over to Burt's after Seth had arrived to start the simple food for Christmas Eve. She was making all kinds of hors d'oeuvre. Dinner would be the next day. She had left the sugar cookies to roll out for this afternoon, everyone pitched in rolling cutting, and decorating the cookies. Her newly acquired best friend, Burt's five year old granddaughter came to sit on her lap. She whispered in Lorinda's ear, "Grandpa bought you a rock for Christmas, don't tell anyone I told you, but I think that's a dumb present."

Christmas Eve finally came, Burt's family and Lorinda's family were instant friends especially the young people.

After everyone had opened their gifts, Burt stood up and announced he had something special to say. He kneeled in front of Lorinda with the biggest diamond she had ever seen and asked her to marry him.

Everyone started clapping and cheering except Lorinda with big tears running down her face she held on to Burt, finally almost speechless she said, "Yes, Yes, Yes!" Her father said, "That's the first time I ever seen my gabby daughter speechless.

Frank and Molly went home, but Seth and Amanda and Burt's young adults started playing monopoly and ended sleeping on the floor by the tree.

When Lorinda got up the next morning her heart was so full she could hardly contain herself and then to see most of her beloved family asleep like little kids all together, she couldn't believe it. Burt got up looked around, "Well you might say our kids sure like each other, for crying out loud there's how many bedrooms in this big house??" Standing with a cup of coffee while Lorinda started breakfast he said, "I don't want you to go home let's just get married and I'll send a truck after your furniture, Please I don't want to spend another day by myself here." Lorinda laughed, "Well Mr. Wonderful, I have something to tell you, I already put in for a transfer to Rapid City's Retail Store and I will start work there in one month, so you bet you will be sending a truck." Burt whirled her around and around, "How did you know?" She laughed, "I was going to ask you to marry me if you didn't get around to it. I don't want to waste another day of my life without you, besides mischief in her eyes, Dad said "He can't afford to feed those damn fish anymore I'd better come home and take care of them.

After all the excitement over Christmas the house seemed too quiet for Burt and Lorinda. They were looking forward to Jim and Marge's wedding the next night. Lorinda's folks were going too, only not for the dance so they were not riding together.

CHAPTER 44

MARGE WAS SO EXCITED about her upcoming marriage she kept pinching herself to see if it as a dream.

She was moving a few boxes every day out to Jim's ranch and getting her house ready to sell. She had put a simple announcement in the local paper inviting everyone in town. She was making a lot of the food at home for the reception and the diner where she used to work was donating the cake and all the paper products.

The night of the wedding she could hardly think, both her and Jim were excited. When she got to the church with Jim's daughter helping her dress she looked out at the crowd gathering in the church and nearly fainted. It looked like the whole town had come and there was Lorinda and her folks and Burt. Blake Denton came to the dressing room and asked to see her, he had brought a special gift just for her. She introduced Jim's daughter and then hugged Blake whispering, "I wish Joel were here, he would be happy for me I know, does it seem awful to you to be so happy when I've lost my only child? "Absolutely not", Blake said, "And I hear your Dad is walking you down the aisle. I'm so happy for you." Marge asked, "Please tell me Julie came too."

Marge woke a bright red dress, walking with her father to meet Jim was a whole church silent until after the vows, the audience went wild. At the reception Burt, Lorinda, Julie and Blake sat together. Lorinda asked Julie about Dale Schultz, Laura had told them that Julie went to see him for Christmas. Julie said, "You won't believe this, but he seems to like it in jail!!!! He told me that he loved Vanna, but for thirty years he never got to sit down and read a book, even a nap was sinful to Vanna, who insisted they work from dawn to dark. He admitted he was kind of enjoying reading doing puzzles and taking a nap when he wanted." Tears in her eyes Julie went on, "You won't believe this, I still can't comprehend the fact that the two of them had a will and I am to receive what's left after the government goes through it all. At first I thought so what then I found out it's a lot of money. I feel strange bout all this and just wish it was over." Blake said, "She's going to marry me even though she will be a rich woman.' Julie explained that Dale signed over the ranch land to her and she wanted to get rid of it as fast as she could sell it. Lorinda held her hand out, with the rock, by now Marge was there too. Julie and Marge hugged Lorinda who said, "Well Julie I'm going home next week to sell my house and get ready to move to Burt's. I called a real estate agent and they tell me my house is worth quite a bit, we'll see, anyway Burt and I could use that to buy your place." Burt looked at Lorinda, "When did you think this up . . . Ah . . . Wow! That would be wonderful, except what about your underground watering system?" Lorinda laughed, "Maybe we can get that after we get rich."

By now everyone was crowding around Lorinda looking at her lovely ring. "When's the wedding? Burt said, "Tomorrow if I have my way!" Frank O'Malley went, "I'm all for that, the sooner you get my girl home, the better I will be satisfied." Marge asked, "If they were having a wedding both Burt and Lorinda in unison said, "No."

Frank and Molly went home, but Burt, Lorinda, Blake and Julie, danced the night away in the local lounge.

CHAPTER 45

LAURA DROVE TO MINNEAPOLIS for New Years' weekend. She met Pete at his small apartment in the city, after stopping for a few supplies they headed for Pete's cabin. They went snow mobile riding and ice fishing. On the last day they both hated the idea of going back to their regular lives. Pete said, "I am going to retire sometime soon and I still want a place in the Black Hills, so . . . ah . . . we could see each other more often." When Laura drove off, looking back she thought he's got tears in his eyes; we hardly know each other for goodness sake. She called Julie when she got home and all excited, breathless described her trip. Julie nearly collapsed laughing, "Mom you sound like you're in love, oh, I hope so, you deserve to be truly happy." Laura scoffed, "It's more like two old people who have a lot.

In the spring after Pete and Laura had talked everyday on the phone he showed up at her house unexpected he said, "Guess what I am officially retired!" After he settled in the kitchen, smelling her homemade bread, he said, "I enjoyed your wonderful baking when I was here last year, running his hands threw his neat hair, ah . . . Laura I can't get you off my mind." She said, "Pete do you still want to buy a nice country house?" "Well, yeah, I've been calling around." Then she said, "Buy mine and—guess what—I come with it." Mr. proper Pete went wild. He picked her up and swung her in the air, "Dear God, I can't tell you in the right words, you know you read about true love and I always thought baloney, but, Oh, Laura, I don't want to live without you, no matter how corny that sounds.

ABOUT THE AUTHOR

MISS LILLIAN WAS BORN and raised on a western South Dakota cattle ranch. She married a farmer from eastern South Dakota where she still lives.